D1006305

PHANTOM ANGEL

Also by David Handler

FEATURING BENJI GOLDEN

Runaway Man

FEATURING BERGER & MITRY

The Coal Black Asphalt Tomb
The Snow White Christmas Cookie
The Blood Red Indian Summer
The Shimmering Blond Sister
The Sour Cherry Surprise
The Sweet Golden Parachute
The Burnt Orange Sunrise
The Bright Silver Star
The Hot Pink Farmhouse
The Cold Blue Blood

FEATURING HUNT LEIBLING

Click to Play

FEATURING STEWART HOAG

The Man Who Died Laughing
The Man Who Lived by Night
The Man Who Would Be F. Scott Fitzgerald
The Woman Who Fell from Grace
The Boy Who Never Grew Up
The Man Who Cancelled Himself
The Girl Who Ran Off with Daddy
The Man Who Loved Women to Death

FEATURING DANNY LEVINE

Kiddo
Boss

PHANTOM ANGEL

DAVID HANDLER

THOMAS DUNNE BOOKS
ST. MARTIN'S MINOTAUR
NEW YORK

This is a work of fiction. All of the characters, organizations, and events portrayed in this novel are either products of the author's imagination or are used fictitiously.

A THOMAS DUNNE BOOK FOR MINOTAUR BOOKS.
An imprint of St. Martin's Publishing Group.

PHANTOM ANGEL. Copyright © 2015 by David Handler. All rights reserved. Printed in the United States of America. For information, address St. Martin's Press, 175 Fifth Avenue, New York, N.Y. 10010.

www.thomasdunnebooks.com
www.minotaurbooks.com

Library of Congress Cataloging-in-Publication Data

Handler, David, 1952-
Phantom angel : a Benji Gold mystery / David Handler.—First edition.
P. cm.—
"A Thomas Dunne Book."
ISBN 978-1-250-05973-4 (hardcover)
ISBN 978-1-4668-6507-5 (e-book)
I. Title.
PS3558.A4637P48 2015
813'.54—dc23

2014034044

Minotaur books may be purchased for educational, business, or promotional use. For information on bulk purchases, please contact the Macmillan Corporate and Premium Sales Department at 1-800-221-7945, extension 5442, or write to specialmarkets@macmillan.com.

First Edition: February 2015

10 9 8 7 6 5 4 3 2 1

This one's for Murder Ink, the Black Orchid,
Foul Play, and all of Gotham's other dear, departed bookshops
that welcomed me and made me feel like I belonged.

PHANTOM ANGEL

CHAPTER ONE

THE GREAT MORRIE FRANKEL LIVED, and worked, in a two-bedroom suite on the eighth floor of the Morley, an elegantly seedy residential hotel that was four doors down West 44th Street from the vastly more famous Algonquin. The Morley was popular with actors from London who were appearing on Broadway in limited run engagements. Also with old-time New Yorkers who like hotel living, which is to say maid service and twenty-four-hour room service. Its bright green awning was tattered. Its lobby smelled musty. So did the eighth-floor corridor. The carpeting, which was of a floral pattern that was quite the rage in the 1940s, was fraying.

The great man himself answered the door when I knocked. Morrie Frankel was a large, overstuffed animal of a man in his sixties with bulging eyes and loose, rubbery lips. His close-cropped salt-and-pepper hair grew unusually low on his forehead. His full beard was cropped the same length as his hair. The effect was, well, Morrie Frankel looked a whole lot like Curious George. There, I said it. He was wearing a bright blue nylon jumpsuit that zipped up the front. For some reason, he also wore a two-inch strip of Scotch tape across his forehead.

He stood there in the doorway looking me up and down with keen-eyed disapproval. Which seemed unfair. It was nine o'clock sharp. I'd shaved and combed my hair. I was wearing my very best pair of four-year-old madras shorts from the Gap, a stylishly untucked white oxford button-down shirt and my black Converse Chuck Taylor high-tops. It was a totally acceptable ensemble for Day Three of the Heat Wave of the Century. The thermometer was supposed to hit 103 degrees by midafternoon.

"*You're* Benji Golden?" he harrumphed at me. "Golden Legal Services?"

"Yes, sir. I am."

He puffed out his cheeks in disbelief. And when I say he puffed them out I'm talking about the way Dizzy Gillespie used to puff his out. Mind you, I've gotten used to this sort of treatment. I'm a quarter inch under five-feet-six, weigh a buck thirty-seven and am exceedingly baby-faced. I look quite a bit younger than my age, which is twenty-five. Then he heaved a huge sigh—absolutely nothing that Morrie Frankel did was small—and said, "Fuck it, you may as well come in."

There was a faux fireplace in the living room. The chintz-covered sofa and matching chairs were quite worn. But the air-conditioning worked. And the gallery of framed, autographed photos of Broadway luminaries, past and present, that lined the walls made my jaw drop. There were photos of Gielgud and Richardson, Tandy and Cronyn, Alec Guinness, Stephen Sondheim, Neil Simon, Carol Channing, Barbra Streisand.

Morrie was right there in each and every photo. Middle-aged Morrie. Young Morrie. There was even a photo of pimply schoolboy Morrie standing with his arm around my own personal idol.

He noticed me gaping at it. "You're a fan of her work?"

"I think Ethel Merman was the single greatest musical comedy star we've ever had. She was the best."

"The best," Morrie agreed. "That picture was taken in 1970 when she was starring in *Hello, Dolly!*, which had already been running for six years. She was the seventh actress to play the role. Way, way past her prime. Or so everyone thought. Believe me, she wasn't. She did two hundred and ten performances. My mom flacked the show." Morrie's mother had been a legendary Broadway publicist, Panama Hattie Frankel. They called her Panama Hattie because of the trademark big white hat she always wore. He gazed at me curiously. "You're an Ethel Merman fan. You look like you should be folding T-shirts at an Old Navy. Ninety percent of the women in New York City would kill for your eyelashes. What kind of a private investigator are you anyhow?"

"The newest kind. I'm honored to meet you, Mr. Frankel. I've enjoyed so many of your shows."

"I appreciate you saying that. Want any breakfast?" He plopped down on the sofa and started attacking his—a giant salad bowl full of what appeared to be sliced bananas and sour cream.

"I'm fine, thanks."

I sat down and watched him eat. I'd been thrilled when I found out that *the* Morrie Frankel wanted to see me. He was the last of the great Broadway showmen, a hands-on independent producer who'd been staging hugely successful musicals out of his back pocket for nearly forty years. He'd made his mark early on by reviving vintage hits starring old-timers who'd supposedly seen better days. It was Morrie Frankel who'd brought an elderly Rex Harrison back to Broadway in a triumphant production of *My Fair Lady*. Also a creaky Richard Burton in a wildly successful *Camelot*. The man had no office to speak of. I was sitting in it. And no corporate backing. He was a throwback, a lone operator who took sole responsibility for staging every one of his shows. For financing he relied upon a highly prized stable of rich, star-struck backers—angels, as they're known on Broadway. He was also a famously volatile bully who possessed a law degree from Columbia and the scruples of a pro-wrestling promoter. Morrie Frankel fought with his directors and his stars, with drama critics, with everyone. Popular legend had it that his walls were papered with lawsuits. They weren't, I can report. Just plain old wallpaper. It was peeling slightly.

A phone rang in another room. I heard a woman answer it, speak briefly, then hang up.

"Hey, Leah . . . ?!"

"What . . . ?!"

"Come out here a sec! Somebody I want you to meet!"

Out came a small, thin woman in her sixties, the kind of woman who is impolitely called birdlike. Since I don't like to be impolite, I'll call her trimly built. She had bobbed silver hair, jet-black brows and very alert brown eyes. She wore a pressed linen dress and gave off an air of tightly wound efficiency.

"Benji Golden, say hello to Leah Shimmel, the best theatrical assistant on Broadway. I'd be lost without her. My enemies have been trying to woo her away for years. They've offered her money, fancy titles, muscular boys. But she'll never leave me. That's because she loves me. Right, Leah?"

Leah responded by yanking that strip of Scotch tape from Morrie's forehead. On his yelp of pain, she barked, "I've *told* you never to wear that when you have company."

"But it keeps those awful frown lines away."

"You look like a putz."

"Oh, who asked you?" he snarled, hurling his bowl of sliced bananas and sour cream at her.

His aim wasn't very good. It shattered against the wall, the bananas and sour cream oozing their way slowly down, down toward the carpet. There were, I noticed, numerous discolorations on the wall. Clearly, Morrie liked to throw things.

And, just as clearly, Leah was accustomed to it. Not at all fazed. "Pleased to meet you, Benji. Feel free to contact me if I can be of any help." She turned on her heel and went darting back to her office.

I had now met the entire staff of Morrie Frankel Productions.

Morrie grabbed a Scotch tape dispenser from the coffee table, yanked off a fresh two-inch strip and smacked it defiantly onto his forehead. Then he sat back and said, "They tell me you're the best in New York when it comes to finding missing young people. There's someone who I'm trying to find. It has to do with my new show, *Wuthering Heights*. Maybe you've heard about it?"

"Who hasn't?"

Morrie Frankel's lavish fifty-million-dollar musical adaptation of Emily Brontë's classic novel of doomed young love had been the juiciest tabloid story on Broadway for months. And was, quite possibly, the biggest unfolding disaster in the disaster-riddled history of the Great White Way. Somehow, he'd managed to sign Matthew Puntigam and Hannah Lane, the hottest young lovebirds in Hollywood, to play Heathcliff and Cathy. Lately, they'd been steaming up the 3-D big screen as the sexiest Tarzan and Jane in movie history. Fresh off of their third straight Tarzan mega-blockbuster the young stars were hungry to conquer the Broadway stage. But trouble kept plaguing *Wuthering Heights*. During a rehearsal of the climactic rainstorm scene Hannah slipped on the rain-soaked set and broke her ankle, which had delayed the opening from last spring to this coming fall. Maybe. As soon as walkthroughs resumed, Morrie had gotten into a highly publicized fistfight at Joe Allen's with his director, three-time Tony Award winner Henderson Lebow, and fired him. They were currently suing each other over how much Morrie was or wasn't contractually obligated to pay him. Supposedly, the show's choreographer was taking over as director. But there were whispers around town that the two young film stars, who had no professional singing experience whatsoever, still couldn't quite carry off the musical's climactic power ballads. Rumor had it that the show's budget might actually climb north of sixty-five million dollars by the time it opened. Rumor also had it that Morrie, who flatly refused to accept a penny of backing from Panorama, the Hollywood studio that had made billions from the Tarzan trilogy, had leveraged every asset he owned to keep his teetering production afloat. And that if he didn't find himself another deep-pocketed angel very soon he might go down. And take *Wuthering Heights* with him.

He studied me from across the coffee table with his bulging eyes. "I'm going to be totally honest with you, okay?"

I nodded politely. My experience has been that whenever people say those words to me that they're getting ready to start lying.

"*Wuthering Heights* isn't just another musical for me. I've dreamed of doing this show ever since I was twelve. That's how old I was the first time I saw the movie with Laurence Olivier and Merle Oberon on the late show. When she went running out into that rain and cried out 'Heathcliff . . . ! Heathcliff . . . !' I swear to you, I cried so hard there was a puddle of tears at my feet. I'm in love with *Wuthering Heights*. Want to know why? Because I'm a romantic. Ask any of my three ex-wives. Or maybe *don't* ask them. They all detest me. Never put your work ahead of a woman's love, young fellow, because she won't understand. She'll say she does, but she won't." He heaved another of his huge sighs. "When I undertook this show I knew right away that I had to have Matthew and Hannah. They *are* Heathcliff and Cathy. He's a brooding scruff, not to mention an actual Brit. And she's so angelic that all you have to do is spend ten seconds with her and you're gaga. They're as excited about *Wuthering Heights* as I am. Deep down inside, they don't just want to be movie stars. None of the great ones do. They want to be up there on a Broadway stage holding an entire theater full of people transfixed by the sheer force of their talent. Once I had them on board I was able to pull out *all* of the stops." Morrie climbed to his feet now, with some difficulty, and began to galumph his way around the living room, his eyes gleaming with excitement. "I've built the single greatest set in Broadway history. There's a multi-level path that winds all the way across the moor from Cathy's house to Penistone Crags, their childhood castle. We use real stone, real soil and real heathers. You can *smell* those damned heathers. And when she goes running after Heathcliff in the rain? We are talking about a rainstorm like no one's ever seen onstage before. My set designer had to literally invent new machinery. It's *really* raining up there. Hannah's *really* getting soaked to the skin in that see-through nightgown of hers. Yet the orchestra and front row don't get so much as a breath of mist on them. And the pumps that recirculate all of that water in the sprinkler system don't make a sound. Audiences today want to be wowed. Trust me, they *will* be wowed. And the music? I promise you, people will be singing 'You're Still My Queen' thirty years from now. And there won't be a dry eye in the house when Hannah breaks into 'I Dreamt I Was In Heaven.' Grown men will weep, Benji. Weep, I'm telling you."

"Is it true that you're not happy with your stars' singing voices?"

He waved me off. "That's a nasty rumor planted by someone who hates me. I have many enemies. That's because I do things my own way. When you do a Morrie Frankel show you get Morrie Frankel. Some people can't handle that. The kids are going to be fine. They're working with a voice coach on their breathing and stamina. Naturally, we'll have to mike them. The Merrick's the hugest theater on Broadway. More than two thousand seats.

We have to mike everybody nowadays. God doesn't make voices like Ethel Merman's anymore. Ethel Merman they could hear in Secaucus. But I have high hopes for Matthew and Hannah. Am I rough on them? You bet I am. I don't coddle my stars. Six months ago I told Hannah that she had to get into a dance studio and learn how to move onstage. Did she listen to me? No. She was too busy steam cleaning her karma. So what happens? She falls down during a rehearsal and breaks her ankle. Would that have happened if she'd listened to me? Never. Did I tell her off? You bet I did. Because she put us on the shelf with me bleeding money. Hannah's a spoiled kid. So is Matthew. But they're starting to understand what's expected of Broadway stars. And they're relishing the opportunity to show the world what they can do. They're performers, after all. And performers yearn to perform."

I was well aware of this. I'd yearned to perform myself. Went to NYU drama school. Did a couple of episodes of *Law & Order*, a week on a soap, a few commercials. But I soon discovered that there isn't much demand for a twenty-five-year-old juvenile type. Make that any demand. So I'd ended up in the family business. "How may Golden Legal Services help you, Mr. Frankel?"

He positioned his pudgy self in front of the sofa just so, then sank slo-o-owly back down onto it. Watching Morrie Frankel touch down on that sofa was like watching someone trying to land the Goodyear Blimp. He settled there, choosing his words carefully. "I'm in big trouble, Benji. The worst kind of trouble a guy like me can get into." He looked at me warily. "You people are discreet, right?"

"We don't go blabbing to Page Six or Cricket O'Shea, if that's what you're wondering. If we did we wouldn't stay in business very long."

"So everything I tell you is confidential?"

"Yes, sir. Absolutely."

"It better be," he warned me. "The truth is, I've been financing this entire show on a shoeshine and a smile for the past three months. I owe *everybody* money. My cast, my set designer, my costumer, you name it. I've got over a hundred people on the payroll who I can't pay. I'm tapped out, Benji. The banks won't lend me another nickel, even though I've signed over to them all of the royalties on every show I've ever produced. I've sold the summer house in Sag Harbor that my mom bought back in 1957. I've sold my winter house in Key West. I have nothing left to sell. And nowhere left to turn. That vampire who runs Panorama Studios, Ira Gottfried, would be happy to bail me out. He's wanted a piece of this show since day one. Matthew and Hannah are his gold mine. And he expects to film *Wuthering Heights*. It'll be an epic movie musical. Huge. But I'll never, ever give Count Dracula a piece of *my* show. It's a Morrie Frankel production. It's *mine*. That's how I operate, for better or worse. Maybe I'm a dinosaur. Maybe I'm crazy. Maybe . . ." He trailed off, clearing his throat uneasily. "Maybe I'm slipping. I entered into a financial relationship with a new backer a couple of weeks ago, and well, I would never have gotten myself into something like this in the old days. But I'm tapped out, like I said. And he seemed so legit."

"Who are we talking about?"

"A slick young hedge fund billionaire named R. J. Farnell."

"R as in Robert, Richard . . . ?"

"I honestly don't know. He's a Brit, maybe thirty-five years old. Loves the theater. Is crazy about *Wuthering Heights*. And he promised he'd advance me the twelve million that I've got to have if I'm actually going to open."

"I saw an item about him on Cricket O'Shea's Web site. She called him 'that noted theatrical benefactor John Q. Somebody.'"

"That's because I wouldn't tell her his name. R.J. wants his identity kept under wraps."

"Why?"

"How would I know why?" Morrie blustered. "He wants what he wants, and I'm respecting it. I need the guy's money. R.J. looked me right in the eye, shook my hand and promised he'd give it to me. As a good faith gesture he even handed me a hundred thou in cash."

"Is that unusual?"

"Is what unusual?"

"Cash."

"Not in this business," Morrie said with a shake of his head. "R.J. assured me he'd be sending me a certified check for twelve mil by messenger by the end of the week. I'm talking about *last* week, Benji. I was counting on that money. I went ahead and made promises to certain people. My landlord, just for starters. That theater costs me a fortune to hold on to. And my newest angels. I've landed some solid new investors thanks to the promise of R.J.'s twelve mil. Just in the past forty-eight hours I've connected with a garment industry exec and another guy who's the founder and president of the second-largest denture adhesive company in North America. They've verbally committed one mil apiece. But if R.J. doesn't come through . . ." Morrie's face dropped. "And he hasn't. In fact, he's disappeared. The phone numbers he gave me have been disconnected. He's moved out of his house. The bastard's *gone*."

"How did you hook up with him in the first place?"

"He called me up. We spoke several times on the phone. He seemed highly intelligent, very charming and very serious about committing money to my show. He invited me out to his place in East Hampton for lunch, so I went."

"When was this?"

"Two weeks ago, like I said. He had a beautiful home on Lily Pond Lane. Beach view, swimming pool, the works."

"Describe him for me, please."

"Okay, sure. He's tall and good looking, with slicked back hair and a three-day growth of beard. Not lacking in the self-confidence department, if you read me. Knows a lot about vintage sports cars and sailboats. His accent, I would say, defies categorization. Sometimes he sounds like he's out of Eton and Cambridge, other times like he has no breeding at all. He told me he'd moved here from London to make his fortune. Left Goldman Sachs a few years back to start his own hedge fund, the Venusian Society." Morrie paused, letting his breath out slowly. "Benji, I can smell a phony from a mile away. I honestly thought R.J. was the genuine goods. Maybe a teeny tiny bit on the shady side, but genuine."

"Back up a second, please. Shady as in . . . ?"

Morrie made a sour face at me. "It's not like the old days. My angels used to be people of genuine class. I'm talking A-list Park

Avenue dowagers in diamonds and furs. These days, I deal with people who call themselves 'entrepreneurs' and 'venture capitalists.' People who get rich by moving other people's money around. I don't know where that money comes from. And I don't want to know. I'd take money from Pol Pot if it meant that *Wuthering Heights* would open."

"I think Pol Pot's dead."

"Oh, yeah? Well, that's going to be me if you can't save me."

"Didn't you have someone check Farnell out?"

"Like who?" he demanded.

"Your lawyer, your accountant . . ."

"*I'm* a lawyer. And I do my own books. Leah did check out the Venusian Society's Web site, which looked totally legit. It was filled with all sorts of testimonials from real life investors who'd made millions by investing with him and . . . God, this sounds so pathetic when I say it out loud, doesn't it? You're absolutely right. I should have done a more thorough job of vetting him. But I was desperate. R.J. threw me a lifeline. I grabbed it. Now he's yanked it away. I don't know where he went. And I don't know why. I don't know a goddamned thing, except that if you don't find him—and my twelve mil—I'll be finished as a Broadway producer."

"You met him only that one time in East Hampton?"

"Yeah, that's right."

"You communicated the rest of the time by phone?"

"Yeah." With a grunt he reached for a bulging leather address book on the coffee table, removed a slip of Morley Hotel notepaper and handed it to me. On it he'd scrawled two phone numbers. One had a 646 New York City area code, the other an East Hampton 631.

"How about e-mail?"

"I don't like e-mail. I prefer to talk to people."

"Did you talk to anyone else who he's connected with?"

"His girlfriend."

"So there's a girlfriend?"

Morrie nodded. "A little blonde who looks good in a bikini. She's young. No more than eighteen, nineteen years old."

"Do you remember her name?"

"Jonquil Beausoleil. That's not a name you forget. She calls herself Boso. Has a slight Southern accent. Comes from . . . Charleston, maybe? One of those places."

"What else can you tell me about her?"

Morrie shrugged his soft shoulders. "She's a showbiz tartlet. A nothing. You throw a stick on Jones Beach and you'll hit a hundred just like her. She was desperate for a part in *Wuthering Heights*. Even slipped me her headshot. Dense I am not. R.J. never said the words out loud but I figured she was attached to the twelve mil. So I promised I'd audition her for an understudy role." He turned his head and bellowed, "Hey, Leah . . . ?!"

"What . . . ?!"

"Bring me a headshot for a girl named Jonquil Beausoleil, will ya?"

"Jonquil *who*?"

"Beausoleil!"

"Gimme a sec! I have to find it!"

"And did you audition her?" I asked Morrie.

"Couldn't."

"Why not?"

"She's disappeared, too."

"I see . . ."

"I asked around, Benji, and everyone says you're the best there is at finding missing girls."

"And boys."

"Excuse me?"

"I also find boys."

"R.J. couldn't keep his eyes, or his hands, off of this girl. I'm no expert at what you do, but it seems to me that if you can find her you'll find him."

"So you still think he's for real?"

Morrie's face tightened. "He has to be."

"If he is then why'd he disappear on you?"

"That's what I'm paying you to find out."

Leah appeared with the headshot, glaring at the fresh piece of Scotch tape on Morrie's forehead. But she didn't yank this one off. Just handed me the headshot and went back in her office.

Jonquil Beausoleil was pretty in what casting agents call a California-girl way. Her long blond hair was parted down the middle. Her smile was sunny and playful. Her eyes were wide set. Except I saw something in those eyes that I recognized. And didn't like one bit. It made me shudder involuntarily. "You said you saw her in a bikini. Does she have any ink or piercings?"

He had to think about it. "Yeah, she has a tattoo of a sunflower on the top of her foot. Her left one, I think. I don't understand why you kids do that to yourselves."

The headshot was of professional quality. I turned it over, but there was no mention of who'd taken it. Or an agency listing for

Jonquil Beausoleil. The only info on the back was her name and phone number.

"You tried calling this number?"

"It's been disconnected."

"Does Actors' Equity know anything about her?"

"Actors' Equity has never heard of her. Can you can find her?"

"I can find her, Mr. Frankel. But let's be clear about one thing. I can't guarantee you that I'll find your twelve million. Do you understand?"

"No, I *don't* understand! I've been doing this for forty years and I've never had an angel leave me holding the bag like this. Why would someone want to do this to me?"

"Just exactly how conniving and ruthless is Ira Gottfried of Panorama?"

Morrie raised an eyebrow at me, or tried. The Scotch tape wouldn't let him. "Why, what are you thinking?"

"You said he'd love nothing better than to be your partner in *Wuthering Heights*. Is there any chance he might engineer something like this to force your hand?"

"More than a chance," he acknowledged.

"Who else wants you to fail?"

"That lying, two-faced bastard Henderson Lebow."

"Your director?"

"*Ex*-director."

"Who else?"

"Plenty of people."

"Like who?"

"Like the other producers in town. The big boys with the deep pockets. Take a stroll up and down the theater district. Study the marquees. Each and every one of those hit musicals will start losing fannies on a nightly basis once *Wuthering Heights* opens. My show will be *the* hottest ticket on Broadway and they know it. It'll cost those greedy bastards millions."

"Are you saying they may have colluded against you to bury *Wuthering Heights*?"

"It wouldn't be the first time that's happened. This isn't a gentlemanly business, Benji." He tilted his head at me curiously. "You think I'm being a paranoid nut, don't you?"

"I'm thinking it sounds awfully elaborate. Also expensive. You told me Farnell coughed up a hundred thou. That's a lot of money."

"Not to them it isn't. Speaking of money, your employer mentioned something on the phone about a retainer in the form of a certified check for five thousand. My personal check will be just as good, won't it?"

"No, it will not."

He glowered at me with those bulging eyes of his. "Are you serious?"

"Totally."

"Well, then how about cash? Do you accept cash?"

I treated the great Morrie Frankel to my most earnest smile. "Cash is always welcome."

THE AIR-CONDITIONING on the New York City subway system is so much more reliable now than it was back when I was a little kid. These days it only breaks down on rare occasions.

Like, say, in August when it's really, really hot out.

I was drenched with sweat by the time I got off of the No. 1

train at Broadway and West 103rd Street. And I could still smell the brothy armpits of the 300-pound guy in the tank top who'd been squeezed in next to me in the crowded subway car. It was a sticky ninety-eight degrees outside now. The air was thick with moisture, the sky a milky white. The spindly trees in Broadway's center divider looked wilted. So did the people who were trudging slowly along.

The offices of Golden Legal Services are located on the second floor of an 1890s brownstone right there on the corner of Broadway and West 103rd, one flight up from Scotty's twenty-four-hour diner and Pearl's nail salon. My dad, Meyer Golden, was the hero cop who caught Briefcase Bob, the subway serial killer who terrorized New York City back in the early '90s. I was just a toddler back then. And Mom was still getting used to being a Mineola housewife named Abby. When my dad first met her she called herself Abraxas and enjoyed the distinction of being the only Jewish pole dancer in New York City. My dad opened the agency after he retired from the job. Bought the whole building, in fact. He and Mom sold our raised ranch in Mineola and moved in to a floor-through apartment on the fourth floor. Mom went to work for him as an operative. So did I. Working for my dad was how I supported myself while I was trying to make it as an actor. When he died from cancer two years ago, Mom took over the agency. She's a fully licensed PI now, same as I am.

I took the stairs up to our office. I wasn't in the mood to deal with the elevator. Unless you nudge its door open just right you can get trapped in there for hours. It's temperamental. So is the building's plumbing, heating and wiring. It's a tired old building. There are those who might even call it a shithole. I call it home.

Lovely Rita was on the phone at her desk getting tough with a deadbeat client who'd owed us money for the past six months. She and I share the outer office. Rita's a lap dancer buddy of Mom's. She danced under the name Natural Born, which referred to not only her boobage but her flaming red hair. She's just under six feet tall and, at age forty-two, still does wonders to a tight knit top and a pair of slacks. Lap dancing was how Rita put herself through the Rutgers computer science program. Give her a keyboard and ten minutes and she can find out anything about anyone. We'd be lost without Rita. Her no-good husband, Clarence, who used to play outside linebacker for the Jets, is currently serving ten to fifteen at Sing Sing for aggravated assault.

Mom's office door was open so that her rackety window air conditioner could send some semi-chilled air out our way. Her office is very homey. She has a big, old-fashioned walnut desk. A Persian rug on the floor. A comfortably worn leather sofa where Gus, our grizzled black office cat, likes to doze. There's an enormous pre-World War II Wells Fargo safe where we keep our weapons, surveillance equipment and good liquor. Wraparound windows overlook our little stretch of upper Broadway.

"I brought you some cash money, boss," I said, plopping Morrie's retainer down on her desk.

"What a sweet gesture, Bunny," she exclaimed, beaming at me. Mom is pushing fifty now but she's still a MILF, and if you don't know what those initials stand for I'm not going to tell you.

I'll just say she's a strikingly attractive woman with huge dark eyes and major league curves. But she hasn't shown an interest in any man since Dad died. "And what does the illustrious Mr. Morrie Frankel have for us?"

"His twelve-million-dollar angel, a British hedge fund player named R. J. Farnell, has disappeared—and taken the future of *Wuthering Heights* with him. Our best lead is Farnell's girlfriend, a wannabe actress named Jonquil Beausoleil." I fished her headshot from my daypack and put it down on the desk. "Her nickname's Boso. If we find her, we'll find him. Maybe."

Rita sashayed in and had a look at the photo. "She's cute."

I studied Boso's eyes, shuddering once again. "She's okay," I said quietly.

Too quietly. Rita, who knows my darkest secrets, studied me with concern. When my heart got stomped on a few months back, Rita performed an act of genuine human kindness and invited me into her bed. What we had together was very pleasant. Also very brief. Deep down inside she and I are family, not lovers. And, well, there's also the whole age and height discrepancy thing. Rita's now dating a very respectable East Side dentist named Myron. They seem very happy together. I'm still alone, but that's something I'm used to.

"There can't be too many Jonquil Beausoleils in New York City, Rita. See what you and your magic fingers can find out about her, okay? Driver's license, credit cards, employment records. Morrie thinks she's originally from Charleston, although he didn't sound real sure."

"No prob," she said, continuing to study me.

"We're searching for her boyfriend, a Brit named R. J. Farnell."

"R as in Robert?"

"No idea. I do know he runs a hedge fund called the Venusian Society."

"I'll look into it." Rita went striding back to her desk.

"Mom, how'd you like to go to East Hampton today?"

"I'd love to," she said eagerly. "It'll be a pleasure to get out of the city. What am I . . . ?"

"Farnell was living in a schmancy house on Lily Pond Lane as of a couple of weeks ago. He and the girl. That's where Morrie met them."

"Say no more. I'll find me a rich bitch realtor." Mom swiveled in her chair and started trolling for one on her laptop. "I'll say I'm working for the law firm that's representing Mrs. Farnell in the divorce proceedings. That'll get her talking."

There was a tap on our hallway door now and in walked Leah Shimmel, Morrie Frankel's personal assistant, who looked a bit flushed from the heat. Also more than a bit aghast. "There is an extremely old man wandering the hallway in a pair of crusty boxer shorts and nothing else," she informed us in horror.

"That would Mr. Felcher, our tenant in 3-B," I said.

"Shouldn't someone be looking after him?"

"That would be Mrs. Felcher, our tenant in 3-A. It's a long story." After I'd introduced her to Mom and Rita, I said, "How may we help you, Leah?"

Leah cleared her throat uncomfortably. "Actually, I was hoping to explain a few things to you. Could we . . . ?"

I bought her an iced coffee downstairs at Scotty's. I opted for a chocolate milk shake myself. We sat in a booth by the window and watched the pedestrians ooze by, laboring in the heat.

"Morrie thinks I'm getting my hair done," she said, taking a small sip of her iced coffee. The glass trembled in her pale, thin-boned hand. "If he knew I was here talking to you he'd go ballistic. Morrie can't handle the idea of anything going on behind his back. That's not to say he's a bad person, despite what you may have heard. But he *is* a control freak, and conflict is his oxygen. If none exists, he'll create it. He needs enemies. If Morrie were a professional athlete people would call him a great competitor. Since he's a theatrical producer they call him a monster. But he's no monster. He's loyal and sensitive and this situation has hit him hard. He's afraid he's losing his grip."

"Is he?"

Leah narrowed her sharp eyes at me before she gazed back out the window. "I don't know, but I am deeply concerned about him. I've never seen him so upset, and I've known that man for a long, long time. Longer than anyone else. Morrie's a creature of the theater, by which I mean he's a big child. He needs constant looking after by someone who's a grown-up."

"Someone like you?"

She smiled at me, a thin smile that vanished quickly. "He's gotten himself into a real jam, Benji. It's bad. So bad that he was ashamed to admit the cold, hard truth to you."

"The cold, hard truth about what?"

"The hundred thousand that Mr. Farnell gave him as a good faith gesture. I'm the person who put up that money, not Mr. Farnell. Morrie borrowed it from me. I didn't hesitate to give it to him, even though it was the last of my savings. Charlie, my son, has gone through the rest. Charlie's someone who, well, he's had a hard time settling down. Morrie . . . Morrie *needed* to tell you that he got the money from Mr. Farnell. He didn't want you thinking he'd been completely duped by that bastard."

"Did you meet Farnell, Leah?"

She shook her head. "Morrie went out to East Hampton by himself. Morrie's handled all contact with him personally. He's been very insistent about that."

"Is that typical?"

"No, it's not. I typically interact with all of his angels. That's my job."

"What do you make of it?"

"Morrie's had a very hard time of it lately. That's what I make of it." She took another cautious sip of her iced coffee, weighing her words carefully. "That ugly dust-up he had with Henderson Lebow in Joe Allen's? That wasn't creative differences between a producer and his director. That was a lover's quarrel. Morrie caught Henderson two-timing him with another man. Poor Morrie sobbed his heart out in my arms for hours."

"I didn't realize that . . . What I mean is, Mr. Frankel gave me the impression that he was straight. In fact, he went out of his way to mention his three ex-wives."

"Of course he did," Leah responded tartly. "Morrie has spent his whole adult life trying to pass as straight—all because of his mother. Panama Hattie was many things. Tolerant wasn't one of them. So for her, he tried to be straight. That's what a lot of gay men used to do. Maybe they still do. I don't know. I only know that Morrie has been gay ever since we were teenagers together at Stuyvesant High. I lived in Flatbush. Morrie lived in the Morley with Hattie. His dad ran off with a dancer when Morrie was a baby. Hattie raised him by herself in the Morley. Would you believe he's lived in that exact same suite since he was nine years old?" She paused, a fond glow softening her seamed, narrow face. "I had never met anyone like Morrie. He was as mad for the theater as I was. And *so* full of moxie. When he was sixteen he was already planting items in Liz Smith's column for Hattie. He'd take me to see a different show every night. After the curtain we'd go backstage and he'd get his picture taken with the stars. It was all like a dream. I was madly in love with him. But he treated me like a sister, nothing more. It didn't take long for me to figure out why. I was so hooked on the theater that I ended up going to work for Hattie as an assistant publicist, working side by side with him eighteen hours a day. And I'm still around all of these years later. I'm the only family Morrie has had since Hattie passed away. Not that I could ever replace her. She was the great love of his life. And shrewd beyond belief. He's been lost without her. Hasn't had one hit show in the five years she's been gone. And his personal life has been nothing but turmoil. He was discreet and careful while Hattie was alive. Now he's reckless. Everyone knows that you don't fall in love with Henderson Lebow. That man is a player. Also a vindictive son of a bitch. He will *never* forgive Morrie for attacking him in Joe Allen's. This R. J. Farnell business? For all I know it could be Henderson's way of getting even. I wouldn't put it past him. Henderson's nasty. Morrie isn't. He's sweet and vulnerable. He yearns for the blissful, innocent love that Cathy and Heathcliff share in *Wuthering Heights*. That's why he adores the show so much."

"You mentioned your son, Charlie. I take it that you settled down with someone else."

"Phil was a CPA with a big firm down on Wall Street," she said, coloring slightly. "A good, steady man. Steady made for a welcome change after a regular diet of Morrie, who experiences every single human emotion every single day. Joy, misery, anger, jealousy, envy . . ."

"I think you're straying into the Seven Deadly Sins now."

"I married Phil because I wanted a normal life. Kids, a dog, a white picket fence, all of that. But we weren't happy together. Not for long. Because *Morrie* is my life, for better or worse. As soon as Phil realized that, he found someone else and divorced me. He died a couple of years ago."

"And Charlie?"

"He lives in Williamsburg. He's studying to be a chef. He has a good heart. He's a good boy. I call him a boy but he'll be thirty in October."

"Are he and Morrie close?"

Leah shook her head. "Morrie doesn't do that."

"Doesn't do what?"

"Take an interest in other people's lives. He only cares about his latest show. And he can't . . ." She reached across the table now and put her hand over mine, clutching it tightly. "Morrie can't lie to me, Benji. I see right through him. I'm the one person in the world who can. And I'm telling you that he is genuinely terrified. Somebody is trying to *ruin* him."

"You say he's terrified. Is there something else you haven't told me?"

Leah released my hand and reached for her iced coffee, taking another sip. "A pair of apes have started dropping by. Real knuckle draggers."

"What do they want?"

"Money, what else? I'm afraid they might throw him out the window or something."

"Who are they?"

"Morrie won't tell me, but I think they work for one of his backers."

"Which backer, Leah?"

She leaned across the table toward me. "He's known as the angel of last resort."

I stared at her. "Do you mean Joe Minetta?"

"Yes," she acknowledged, her voice barely a whisper.

Joe Minetta was the head of the largest crime family in New York City. He had many legitimate business interests, such as hotel and restaurant linen supplies, private garbage hauling and real estate management. He also had a financial stake in a lot of the city's big-ticket live entertainment—rock concerts, boxing matches, anything and everything including Broadway shows. He got that stake by serving as a loan shark to cash-strapped promoters and producers.

"I'm afraid that Morrie has gotten in over his head with some very dangerous people," Leah said to me in a quavery voice. "But he's blind to it. Convinced that *Wuthering Heights* will be the biggest hit in Broadway history and that all of his money troubles will vanish in a sea of green."

"And what do you think?"

Leah Shimmel's eyes shined at me. "I think if he doesn't come up with some serious money—and fast—that something truly awful is going to happen to him."

CHAPTER TWO

VICKI ARDUINO WAS the busiest casting agent in New York City. She had an amazing knack for finding the perfect person for a feature film or TV role. Also a photographic memory. The woman never forgot a face. Whenever I was searching for a girl like Jonquil Beausoleil—someone who was dreaming the impossible showbiz dream—I went looking for Vicki.

I found her that day at the Hudson Studio, where she was casting day players for an abysmal network sitcom about a male nanny that was going into its fifth season. The Hudson Studio was on West 26th Street over near Ninth Avenue on the edge of the garment district. There were trucks double-parked in the street. Guys in tank tops and shorts were unloading racks of winter coats, the sweat pouring off of them in the poisonous midday heat. The temperature had climbed to 101 degrees. It was so hot out that the blacktop under my feet felt soft as fudge as I scooted my way across the street to the studio, which was housed in a converted brick warehouse. I once shot a Verizon commercial there that went national.

Inside of the double doors there was a tiny reception area, where a young guy wearing a Hudson Studio T-shirt was parked at the desk. I told him I was there for the audition. He let me on through. That line almost always works at a studio because there's almost always an audition going on somewhere.

The phones were ringing nonstop in the sitcom's third-floor production office. Harried production assistants rushed this way and that. I strode briskly through them, my gaze never wavering. No one in a production office will question who you are if you act like you know where you're going. I was going to a lounge area where two-dozen nervous actors in assorted shapes and colors were parked on sofas and chairs and the floor. All were between the ages of forty and sixty. All wore workman's overalls. All chewed gum with their mouths open as they studied their sides.

An office door opened and an actor in overalls came out followed by a PA with a clipboard.

Before the PA could usher in the next actor, I slipped my way inside and said, "Let me guess—you're looking for an apartment super who's between the ages of forty and sixty and chews gum with his mouth open."

Vicki let out a loud guffaw as she sat there at a desk devouring a Big Mac and fries. She was an overweight, disheveled mess of a woman—which never ceased to inspire catty remarks from out-of-work actors. That day she had on a ketchup-spotted black knit ensemble that was too snug in all the wrong places. "Well, if it isn't Benji Golden, pubescent private eye. I still think Dick Wolf should do a show about you."

"You and me both, Vicki. But only if I get to play myself."

The PA stuck her head in and said, "Next we have Mr. Frank Ionelli reading for the part of Joe, the building super."

"Give me one sec, Tina, okay?" The PA left us, closing the door behind her. "Benji, I have a half hour to cast this part before I've got a dozen eight-year-old girls *and* their mothers coming in. What do you need?"

I placed Jonquil Beausoleil's headshot on the desk before her.

Vicki fished her reading glasses out of her overstuffed shoulder bag. They were canary yellow and were missing the right earpiece. Balanced askew on her nose as she peered down at the photo. She took them off and sat back in her chair. "Jonquil Beausoleil. Calls herself Boso. I saw her when I was casting *Royal Pains* back in May."

"And . . . ?"

"Pretty girl. Slight hick accent. *Extremely* slight talent. I was looking for a pair of sorority bimbos. She auditioned with another girl who we liked." Vicki took a bite of her Big Mac, dabbing at a dribble of sauce on her chin with a sodden napkin. "Her we ended up using."

"Did they come to the audition together?"

"No, we just paired them off at random."

"Did Boso have agency representation?"

"She was hoping to get an agent if she got the part."

"How about a modeling agency?"

"Not a chance. She's itsy. No more than five-feet-three."

"Did she mention who she'd been studying with?"

Vicki shook her head. There was, I noticed, ketchup in her uncombed black hair. A lot of ketchup.

"How did she hear about the audition?"

"How do any of you people hear about auditions? The word gets out. Before there was Facebook there were actors."

"Vicki, do you have a current phone number for her? The one I've got is no longer in service."

"I don't have a thing, Benji. And now I have to throw you out."

"You're the best, Vicki."

"Damned straight I am." As I started for the door, Vicki added, "She came to the audition with a guy—tall, handsome, shoulders out to here."

"Did he have a British accent?"

She frowned at me. "Why would he have a British accent?"

"Any idea who he was?"

"I know exactly who he was," she replied. "Farmer John."

"Who's Farmer John?"

"You know him."

"I do?"

"He's famous."

"He is?"

"Yeah, he's been on the news a bunch of times. He's that Park Avenue do-gooder who converted a bunch of abandoned lots in Brownsville into an urban vegetable farm. And, God, what a hunk. Him I could cast in two seconds flat. But the man's not interested. Too busy saving humanity." Vicki Arduino paused to devour a greasy French fry. "One mouthful at a time."

AS I RODE THE NO. 3 TRAIN out to the Brownsville section of Brooklyn, I listened to the original Broadway cast recording of *Annie Get Your Gun* on my iPod and used my laptop to read up on Farmer John, which is to say John Mason Granger III, age twenty-four. There was a whole lot of news coverage about him. He was an All-American rich kid—the only son of John Mason Granger, Jr., managing partner of Granger and Haynes, the big money Wall Street law firm. And he'd been a straight-A student at Yale until he dropped out in the middle of his senior year to launch the Farm Project, an eight-thousand-square-foot urban farm that he'd dug out of the weeds and broken glass in one of the city's most blighted neighborhoods. It hadn't been easy. He'd had to convince the city to grant him the use of the neglected vacant lots. And to run water to them from the water main under the street. That had cost money. So had things like sturdy chain-link fencing, lumber and tons and tons of topsoil and mulch. He'd raised most of the twenty-four thousand dollars that he'd needed from small investors online via Kickstarter. Then rounded up volunteers with strong backs to help him. And enlisted the teachers at the neighboring elementary school, PS 323, to embrace the farm as a so-called Edible Schoolyard where the neighborhood kids could learn about science, math and nutrition by planting seeds, watching them grow and feasting on the fruits of their labors. It had proven to be such a resounding success that it was now a model for future urban farms all across America.

It was on the corner of Rockaway Avenue and Sutter Avenue, across the street from a Laundromat and a bodega. A hand-lettered sign on the open front gate read: *Welcome to the Edible Schoolyard*.

It was startlingly green there. The planting beds were bursting with ripe tomatoes, string beans, eggplants and squashes. It was also bustling. There had to be forty kids and grown-ups harvesting and weeding despite the scorching heat. Nearly all were people of color, with the exception of a handful of volunteers who wore bright green I VOLUNTEERED T-shirts. Teenaged boys and girls were clustered together on benches, chattering away. A laughing little boy stuck a fresh-picked cherry tomato down the back of a little girl's T-shirt and took off running. She let out a shriek and went chasing after him.

Farmer John was not hard to find. He was as strapping and handsome as Vicki Arduino had said. At least six-feet-four, with floppy blond hair and a granite jaw. He wore a pair of denim overalls cut off at the knees and Nikes without socks.

He smiled at me when I approached him and said, "I'm John. Thanks for coming out."

"Glad to be here." I shook his work-roughened hand. "I'm Benji Golden."

"Are you here to lend a hand, Benji?"

"Not exactly. I'm a private investigator."

"You're messing with me, right?"

"No, I'm not. A client has hired me to find Jonquil Beausoleil."

Farmer John's face fell. He pulled a blue bandana from his pocket and wiped the sweat from his forehead. "Is it her mom? Did Boso's mom hire you?"

"That information's confidential, I'm afraid. But why do you ask?"

"Who else would be looking for her? And it's about time, too. Boso took off from there at least four months ago."

"By 'there' you mean . . . ?"

"Ruston, Louisiana. That's where she's from." He studied me curiously. "You don't know much of anything, do you?"

"It's true, I don't."

"Step into my office." He led me over to a shaded area under a canvas overhang. We sat down on a couple of overturned crates and he popped the lid off an ice chest, rummaging around in it. "How about a cold beer?"

"Not right now, thanks."

"Bottle of water then. Got to stay hydrated in this weather."

He removed two bottles of Poland Spring and handed me one.

I unscrewed the top and took a long drink. "You're making quite a go of it here," I observed.

"I've had so much help," he said modestly. "The Central Park Conservancy donated all sorts of shovels and wheelbarrows. Not to mention volunteers to help me clear the land and haul the trash away. The teachers at PS 323 have been incredibly supportive. And would you believe the Department of Sanitation donated over a hundred cubic yards of compost?" He gulped down some water. "It's been a struggle, but just look how much fun these kids are having."

"This is a not-great neighborhood. Do the gangs give you any trouble?"

"None," he replied. "As far as they're concerned I'm like a priest. Somebody who's strictly here to help. A lot of the younger guys even pitch in. That's why I keep a couple of six packs in the cooler. I tell them, hey, if you put in an hour hauling compost you get a beer. It's a win-win." He grinned at me. "Besides, there are a lot of cute girls here. The neighborhood girls are my Summer Stewards. It gives them somewhere to be, and they stay out of trouble here. No drugs are allowed. And the police steer clear unless I reach out, which I don't." He took another gulp of water. "I'd like to build a hen house next so they can have fresh eggs. I'll let you in on a dirty little secret, Benji. Violence isn't the biggest problem in this neighborhood. Poor nutrition is. These people have unbelievably high rates of obesity, high blood pressure and diabetes. A lot of that has to do with what they're eating, which is too much greasy fast food."

Vicki Arduino was right. He was trying to save humanity one mouthful at a time.

"How did you end up doing this?"

"Somebody has to atone for the sins of my father. That's my name on his office door, too, you know. My father's the managing partner of Wall Street's most heinous foreclosure mill. His law firm is on the side of the big banks and mortgage lenders when they kick honest, hardworking people out of their homes. He has hundreds of lawyers working for him. They have no scruples. And they learn everything they know from *him*," he said with cold certainty. "I was supposed to follow in his footsteps. First Yale, then law school, then Granger and Haynes. But I won't be a part of his system. I flew down to Haiti to help the Red Cross dig sanitation ditches for a while. Thought about staying there permanently until it dawned on me that the Third World is right here in New York City thanks to people like my father. The sad reality is that practically everyone has given up on these kids," he said as he watched them frolic in his garden. "I haven't. They're good kids. And they're full of hope—until we take it away from them."

"Did Boso come out here to volunteer? Is that how you met her?"

His face tightened. "Not exactly. I don't spend very much time in Manhattan anymore. My apartment's in Bed-Stuy. But I went home to see my mother one day back in May when my father was away on a business trip. My mother's okay. She doesn't totally understand what I'm doing but she has my back. We had lunch together on the terrace. It was a nice, sunny spring day. I took a walk through Central Park afterward. I found Boso sitting on a bench by the Bandshell with her duffel bag, sobbing her head off. Cutest little thing I'd ever seen in my life. Eighteen years old. Slammin' bod. She's a fitness freak, you know. And a vegan. I asked her if there was anything I could do to help. We talked for a long, long time. She told me she was from Ruston, Louisiana. She calls it *Loozianna* when she loses her temper, which happens a lot. She was supposed to start her freshman year at LSU this fall but she skipped town before she graduated from Ruston High. She was a big time cheerleader there. Won all sorts of national competitions. She has major acrobatic skills. Came up here to try and make it as an actress. When I met her that day in the park she'd hit bottom. Run out of money. Run out of friends' places where she could crash. She was homeless. I told her she could crash on my sofa for a few days if she'd put in some time working here. And so she did. And pretty soon she was sharing my bed with me," he recalled wistfully. "We had a lot of fun together. And she was a huge help here. She knows a lot about gardening from her dad. They were real close. But he suffered from depression. When he found out her mom was involved with another guy he killed himself."

"When was this?"

"About three years ago, I think. Her mom ended up marrying

the guy. Boso never forgave her. She totally hates her mother. Won't even let her know where she is."

"And what about her stepfather?"

"She doesn't talk about him much, other than to say he's an asshole. Boso's someone who has strong feelings about people. She's got a lot of fire in her. She's smart, she's intuitive . . ."

"Is she a sound sleeper? Does she get nightmares?"

He looked at me in surprise. "All of the time. How did you know that?"

"Please continue. You were saying she's smart, she's intuitive . . ."

"And a hard worker," he added, nodding. "She slung drinks for caterers, taught exercise classes, any kind of cash gig she could get. She took a lot of acting classes in the East Village. Went on all sorts of auditions. Boso's super talented. She'll make it. I really believe that. Because she's *genuine*. Most girls I meet aren't. They're layer upon layer of artifice. Not Boso. Her heart is right there. She just reaches in and hands it to you."

"When was the last time you saw her?"

"Two months ago. She told me she'd seen an ad on Craigslist for some agency that was looking for models and actresses."

I felt my stomach muscles tighten. "And . . . ?"

"She met with some guy in midtown who told her he could get her paying work right away as a model. She went back the next morning to have him take some pictures of her and . . ." Farmer John trailed off, his broad chest rising and falling. "And that was the last I saw of her. She never even came back for her clothes. Not that she left much behind. But I keep thinking she'll come back." He gazed at me imploringly. "Do you think she'll come back?"

"I don't know."

"Will you do me a favor if you find her? Will you tell her that I miss her? So does Leon. He's the kitten we got. She loved that little cat."

"Sure, I'll tell her."

He mustered a smile. "Thanks. And come on back any time. I'll put you to work. I'll even buy you that beer. Deal?"

I HAD TWO VOICE MAILS from the great Morrie Frankel on my cell phone. The first one was quite cordial: "Benji? It's Morrie. I was wondering if you've made any progress yet. Call me back, okay?" The second was considerably less so: "Benji? It's Morrie. *Again*. I want to know what's going on. Call me the fuck back, you little pisher!"

My dad taught me to never give a client too many details in the early stages of an investigation. Those details have a way of mutating on you as the hours go by. So I didn't call Morrie the fuck back. Not yet.

I rode the No. 3 from Brownsville back to the Wall Street station, where I joined up with the sweaty mass of subterranean straphangers who were packed in down there like stewed tomatoes waiting for a train, any train. I caught the M, which took me to the Lower East Side. I was in search of a dirty old man.

His name was Phillip J. Barsamian, known by his friends as Philly Joe. Back when I landed two days of work on *Law & Order: Criminal Intent* playing a prep school drug dealer it was Philly Joe who played my weary old public defender. The two of us got to talking between setups and I discovered that way back in the late 1960s Philly Joe had been a hot young Broadway *somebody* who'd scored huge as the goofy kid brother in a hit Neil Simon comedy. From there he'd landed the goofy second lead in an offbeat little Robert Altman film. Goofy was in real demand in those days, and Philly Joe was the clown prince of goofy—tall and gangly with a shock of curly red hair, a huge Adam's apple and such unusually long arms and legs that he resembled an ungainly prehistoric bird. He'd gone out to L.A. to star in a sitcom pilot for Norman Lear that CBS didn't pick up. Was quickly offered a role on the sitcom *Rhoda* but chose instead to return to Broadway to star in a play that folded in a week. And then, before Philly Joe knew what hit him, goofy was out and so was he. Now, forty years later, he was just another struggling actor who worked in his family's business to make ends meet.

His family's business was Helen's, a dairy restaurant that had been selling blintzes, borscht and mushroom barley soup on the same corner of Second Avenue and East 8th Street since the 1930s. Helen had been Philly Joe's grandmother. His brother and sister ran the restaurant now. Philly Joe waited tables there when he wasn't going on auditions, same as he had when he was a teenager.

I was looking for him because Philly Joe happened to be a rather unusual authority. The man devoted every free moment of every day and night to the singular pursuit of watching online porn. This made him someone whom I occasionally found helpful. Like, say, when a guy has just told me that his hot young girlfriend answered an ad in Craigslist and was never heard from again. Philly Joe was, by most people's definition, a perv. But my job brings me into contact with people who are far pervier. Besides, I felt sorry for him. He was a gifted actor who'd flamed out. And he hadn't enjoyed any non-virtual sexual activity since 1982. That was when the last woman who'd been willing to sleep with Philly Joe told him that she'd tried to cope with his cooties but couldn't. There was no denying that he had them. Cooties, that is. There was something just a bit *off* about Philly Joe.

Helen's was doing a brisk business at five o'clock. The Early Bird Special crowd flocked there. So did the Lower East Side's young hipsters. Philly Joe was on the job in a white shirt, black slacks and white apron. He was pushing seventy. His shock of red hair was streaked with gray. But he was still a comically gangly, splay-footed creature as he made his way down the aisle balancing a tray full of borscht. An adroit waiter he was not. Shaky was more like it.

"Hiya, Benji boy," he called to me cheerfully. "Want some dinner?"

"Information, actually. I'm in a position to pay you."

"And I'm in a position to let you. I'll take my break."

He joined me out on the sidewalk a few minutes later, minus his apron. The thermometer was still hovering in the upper 90s, and the humidity was stifling. But we didn't have far to go. Philly Joe lived right around the corner from the restaurant in the same rent-stabilized studio apartment he'd always had. He was a tidy housekeeper. His bed was made. Everything was nice and neat. Just not clean. Philly Joe's apartment had cooties same as he did. It was as if he'd polished the furniture with earwax.

He'd left the window air conditioner set on low. He cranked

it up to high and parked himself at his round oak dining table, which was anchored by a twenty-seven-inch Mac desktop computer. "Who have we got?" he asked, stretching and popping his fingers like a pianist preparing to play a concerto.

I passed him Boso's headshot and sat in the chair next to his. Not too close.

He squinted at it, twitching his busy beak of a nose. "Hmm . . . Her face isn't much to go on. There are an awful lot of girls who look like this. Any tats?"

"A sunflower on her left foot."

Now Philly Joe raised his eyebrows at me. "Are you sure it's not her right foot?"

"I'm not sure of anything. Why, do you know her?"

"I might, my young friend. I just might. You know who I'm thinking of? Sweet young Cassia. Also known as Lisa B and Eva E. These girls go by a million aliases, which I don't have to tell the man whose mom used to call herself Abraxas. What's this sweetie's real name?"

"Jonquil Beausoleil. She calls herself Boso. Have you seen her?"

"Oh, I've seen her. I never forget a rosebud. And this girl has herself a real beaut." He started tapping away at his keyboard. "Hmm . . . She doesn't have her own Web site yet. Not under any of her aliases. Is she new at this?"

"Been at it less than two months."

"Still getting her dainty feet wet. In that case . . ." He tapped away some more. "Yeppers, here she is. She's listed as Cassia on *sweetgirls.com* and as Lisa B and Eva E on *babesalone.com*. Those are both so-called good girl sites. Nothing more than modeling and webcams. In the world of hardcore that makes her a virgin—unless she's also hooking on the side, which at least half of them are. But why go there? It'll just depress us. . . . I'm finding two photo galleries and one video. Ready to check her out?"

A gallery of twelve color photographs came up on his computer screen. He converted it to a slide show for me. A slide show of Boso sprawled this way and that on a bed wearing a black velvet thong and nothing else—unless you count that tattoo on her right foot. Her long blond hair was tousled. Her big blue eyes promised all sorts of carnal delights. She had an amazingly well-toned little body, just like Farmer John said. And a golden, all-over tan. Rose petals were scattered across the bed in a way that I guess was meant to be artful. The photos were no more revealing than anything you could see in *Playboy*.

"She's some little sweetie, isn't she?" Philly Joe's tongue flicked over his lips in a most unappetizing way. "And all natural, too. Those boobies are a hundred percent real."

The second photo gallery had been shot on the deck of a sailboat at sea. The clear sky and sparkling water were blue. The deck was white. And Boso was oiled up and golden—an All-American dream girl captured in an array of poses that managed to not only demonstrate how limber she was but to offer a dozen different unobstructed views of her hairless hoo-hoo.

Philly Joe sighed contentedly. "Like I said, it's a genuine rosebud."

My eyes scanned the boat for a name or registry, but I found nothing. I also studied the coastline in the distant background. It looked vaguely familiar. "Can I see the video now?"

It was brief, less than two minutes long. Boso was stretched out in a lounge chair applying baby oil to her naked self, rubbing it slowly and seductively over her small breasts and flat stomach. The lounge chair was parked on the balcony of a high-rise hotel or apartment building. There was a planter box behind her and a sliding glass door next to her. She was wearing a pair of mirrored sunglasses, which interested me greatly.

"Can you e-mail me the links to all of those, Philly Joe?"

"On their way as we speak," he assured me, tapping away.

"Tell me about these good girl Web sites. Where do they originate from?"

"Probably some guy's basement in Croatia," he said, sitting back in his chair. "A lot of these girls are from the former Soviet Republics."

"This one's from the republic of Louisiana."

"Really? We have a Louisiana right here in the good old . . . Oh, you're pulling my pud, aren't you, you little wisenheimer."

"What's in it for the guys who run these sites? If you can access this stuff with a click, I mean."

"What we just looked at is considered promo material. They're hoping you'll ante up thirty-nine dollars a month for membership in their Gold Club or Premiere Club or whatever the hell they're calling it. That gets you access to live streaming webcam videos and private online chats. Private sex shows, too, or so they promise."

"You've never antied up?"

"Benji, I'll be seventy years old in a few weeks. There's more free porn available on the Internet than a man my age can shake his stick at, you should pardon the expression." Philly Joe twitched his nose at me again. "Boso's a tasty little piece, my young friend.

It's only a matter of time before she loses her virginity. They'll have to turn her out. Won't be able to help themselves."

"I know that." I set four fifty-dollar bills down on the table. "Are you still going on auditions?"

"Are you kidding? I'll still be going on auditions when I'm on life support. Hey, I hear they may be reviving *The Odd Couple*. Don't you think I'd be a perfect Felix?"

"I think you could play the hell out of Felix."

"Doc Simon liked my work, you know. That's what he said to me when I was in his show. He said 'I really like your work, son.' Did I ever tell you that?"

Honestly? He'd told me that three times. This made four. The old man clung to the playwright's forty-five-year-old compliment like it was a life raft. But I wasn't about to take it away from him. Nope, not me. "You never did, Philly Joe," I said. "That's a hell of a thing."

"A hell of a thing," he agreed, beaming at me as I went out the door and left him there.

"MORRIE FRANKEL HAS PHONED five times in the last two hours," Lovely Rita informed me.

"What did he want?" I said into my cell as I hoofed it westward on East 8th Street.

"*You,* little lamb. He told me you won't return his calls. He used some very naughty words to describe you."

"I hope you defended me."

"I couldn't. I was too busy blushing."

"Got any news for me, Rita?"

"Plenty. For starters, R. J. Farnell's high-flying hedge fund, the Venusian Society, has no assets, no investors and conducts no business of any kind. I checked with a friend of mine who's a lawyer with the SEC. He's never heard of it or of Farnell. Neither has my pal who's a governor of the Federal Reserve." Rita has a lot of Wall Street friends from her lap dancer days. "Real deal? The Venusian Society is nothing more than a name and a Web site. It's bogus. *He's* bogus. Mind you, I have found eighteen R. J. Farnells in the tri-state area, plus another dozen who are listed as Robert J., Richard J., Ronald, Randolph, Rance . . ."

"Rance?"

"I've eliminated ten of them so far, unless you're looking for, say, the manager of a Dunkin' Donuts franchise in Freehold. I'll keep at it, but I'm not feeling very lucky."

"What about those phone numbers that Morrie had for him?"

"Nothing more than disposable cells. His girlfriend, Jonquil Beausoleil, is totally off the grid. No driver's license, no credit cards, no nothing. This is a girl who doesn't want to be found. I can try to back-trace her from Charleston if you—"

"It's not Charleston. It's Ruston, Louisiana."

"Sounds like *you* got somewhere."

"I found her, in a manner of speaking."

"What manner would that be?"

"I just forwarded you two nude photo galleries. Also a video."

"Got 'em. Let's see what we . . . Oh, goodie, here she is on a yacht. Wow, she sure is a limber little thing, isn't she? I could never do a full split like that. Not even when I was on 'ludes. What am I looking for here? Because I've seen a vay-jay before. Although I'm wondering if they Photoshopped hers because it *really* looks like she's wearing lipstick on it, don't you think?"

"I think we're getting off of the subject here. And no."

"Okay, here she is on her tum-tum in a hotel room. What am I . . . ?"

"Any detail, however tiny, that might tell us where she is. When you start enlarging the images you may spot something. An item on that nightstand next to the bed. Or a reflection coming off of a picture on the wall. Maybe you'll be able to make out what's outside the window."

"Want me to check out the yacht, too?"

"Please. And zoom in on that coastline in the background. I could be wrong but it sure looks like the South Shore of Long Island to me."

"I'll see if I can find a landmark. What else?"

"Are you watching the video yet?"

"Hang on . . . Yeah, Boso's rubbing baby oil on her boobies. What about it?"

"Those mirrored sunglasses she has on. I thought I saw an image reflected in them."

"You do realize that you're the only man in the entire world who was looking at her sunglasses, don't you?"

"Can you digitally enhance it?"

"I'll try," she sighed. "But there's only one of me, Benji, and I just broke my umpteenth dinner date with Myron. He got all sore at me about my 'priorities' so I promised I'd meet him for a late supper and . . . did I remember to mention there's only one of me?"

"What I remember is that one of you is more than enough for any man."

"Are you getting frisky with me?"

"What if I am?"

"You need to find yourself a nice girl."

"Yeah, I'll get right on that."

I caught the No. 4 train up to Grand Central, then rode the Shuttle across to Times Square where I was, in fact, looking for a girl. Although the one I was looking for wasn't somebody whom I'd call nice.

The sun was setting by the time I climbed the steps up to 42nd Street. Times Square is no longer the deliciously raunchy Times Square of old with its XXX movie houses, dive bars and sleazy strip clubs. It's now a gaudy Las Vegas-style re-creation of Times Square. Ginormous Diamond Vision TV screens soar one atop another twenty stories into the sky hawking Coca-Cola and Bud Light. There's a Hard Rock Cafe. There's a Levi's store. Families of tourists wearing fanny packs crowd the sidewalks, walking four, six, eight abreast, loaded down with shopping bags. Times Square just doesn't feel like New York anymore. Although on a steamy hot summer night it does still *smell* like New York—that oh-so-distinctive blend of car exhaust fumes, molten blacktop, street vendor hot dogs, maxed-out sewage pipes and decomposing garbage.

It was nearing curtain time, and the sidewalks of the theater district were crowded with people. I took Shubert Alley to West 45th Street and made my way past the Booth, the Schoenfeld, the Jacobs and the Golden, knowing I'd find her eventually. Cricket O'Shea was never anywhere else once evening fell. I walked past the mammoth, shuttered David Merrick Theatre on West 46th, where *Wuthering Heights* had been in rehearsals until Hannah Lane broke her ankle. I tried Joe Allen's, but the bartender there told me he hadn't seen Cricket. I stuck my nose in Bruno Anthony's on Eighth Avenue, hangout of choice for out-of-work actors. No sign of her. Nor at Margot Channing's, the bar across from the Hirschfeld. From there I made my way along West 44th to Zoot Alors, a boisterous Parisian-style bistro that was popular with theatrical agents, flacks and journalists. They were stacked three deep at the hardwood bar and filled the tables under the brightly lit chandeliers. I didn't see her there either, but since Zoot Alors was her favorite haunt I figured she'd end up there eventually. Plus my stomach was growling. So when a barstool opened up I slipped my way onto it and ordered myself a cheeseburger with fries and a glass of milk.

She came hurtling through the door—all four-feet-eleven of her—with her laptop and a fistful of iPhones just as I was biting into my burger. Cricket weighed no more than ninety pounds and had no boobage to speak of. Her pale arms looked like cooked spaghetti in the sleeveless black T-shirt that she was wearing with tight black jeans and a pair of vintage white go-go boots. She had a mountain of black hair tinged with blue, a nose ring and a neck tattoo that read I LOVE THIS DIRTY TOWN—a tribute to J. J. Hunsecker's famous line from *The Sweet Smell of Success*, which is Cricket's all-time favorite movie. We saw it together at the Film Forum when we were freshmen at NYU. She and I were classmates. Cricket started out wanting to act, same as me. She ended up writing about the theater. Covered Broadway for the *Village Voice* before she became sole owner and content provider of *crickoshea.com*, which now ranked as *the* Web site for theater world gossip. If a show was on its way up or on its way down Cricket knew it. If an actor or actress was in trouble, Cricket knew it. She worked nonstop, updated her postings day and night and dug up amazing dirt on Broadway's best and brightest—thanks in part to her live-in boyfriend, Bobby, who was a personal trainer to a number of top stars. Also their pot dealer.

She said hey to the bartender before she spotted me scarfing my cheeseburger and shrieked, "OMG, it's *Benji*!" Low-key Cricket was not. "How *are* you, cutie?" Her cell rang before I could say a word. She took the call. "What's the up? Uh-huh . . . Uh- huh . . . Love it. Love *you*. Later." Rang off and said, "Benji, puh-leeze tell me you're here because you need me."

"I'm here because I need you. Can I order you something?"

"Is somebody else buying?"

"Somebody else is."

"Give me an Irish coffee, Al!" she called out to the bartender.

"Cricket, it's ninety-six degrees outside," I pointed out.

"Doesn't matter. I'm always cold—especially my feet." Her eyes twinkled at me. "As you may remember."

Cricket wasn't just any classmate. She owned my virginity. It was she who'd made the first move. I was kind of shy in those days. Cricket kind of wasn't. "So are you going to fuck me or what?" she'd demanded one night over beers at the White Horse Tavern. So I did. And it wasn't very good. Not unless elbowy, gulpy and rapid-fire are your idea of good. I don't know if it was her fault or mine. I do know that I've been considerably more successful with other women. Not that there have been a lot. Not unless three is your idea of a lot. But Cricket and I just didn't click that way. So we settled for being friends.

Her cell rang again. She took the call and listened a moment before she said, "Already heard about it. Hit me next time, okay?"

Rang off as the bartender brought her the steaming Irish coffee. She took a sip, her tongue flicking the creamy foam from her upper lip. "What can I do for you, cutie?"

"Ever hear of a Broadway angel by the name of R. J. Farnell?"

"Can't say I have because I haven't. Who he?"

I forked some French fries into my mouth, chewing on them. "The guy who's supposed to save *Wuthering Heights*."

She let out a roar of laughter, turning heads. Cricket has mighty large lungs for someone so little. "You mean *Withering Heights* don't you? No one can save that show. It's the biggest disaster in the history of the theater." She peered at me in her inscrutable way. "Please don't tell me you're working for Morrie Frankel."

"Okay, I won't."

"My God, you are, aren't you?"

"What have you heard?"

She crinkled her nose. "Just that Morrie has a John Q. Somebody out there. He won't tell a soul who the guy is. Are you telling me his name's R. J. Farnell?"

"This is strictly between us. You'll burn me if you spread it around."

"I won't," she promised. "Scout's honor."

"Yes, his name's Farnell. He's a British hedge fund billionaire, or claims to be. Has a girlfriend named Jonquil Beausoleil." I pulled out my phone and showed her a photo of Boso on that bed in her black velvet thong.

Cricket studied it carefully. "Don't know her. She's cute."

"She's okay," I said quietly.

Cricket swatted me on the shoulder. "Talk to me, will you? What's the up?"

"Farnell promised to bail Morrie out to the tune of twelve mil. But now he and his twelve mil have vanished, and if Morrie can't find him he's going to lose *Wuthering Heights*—and what's left of his reputation. He'll be done."

"Morrie Frankel is a consummate fucktard. There's no shortage of people who wouldn't mind seeing that happen."

"Like who?"

"Where do you want me to start?"

"With that major dustup he and Henderson Lebow had. Is it true that they actually came to blows in Joe Allen's?"

"It wasn't much of a fight," she sniffed. "Morrie punched him and Henderson belly flopped on somebody's table with his head in their salad Niçoise."

"I hear it was a lover's quarrel."

"You hear right. Morrie found out that Henderson was dogging him with a much younger man."

"Any guesses who that much younger man was?"

"This reporter doesn't have to guess. This reporter knows. Henderson was, and still is, getting it on with loincloth boy himself, as in 'Me Tarzan.' "

"Wait, he's sleeping with Matthew Puntigam?"

"Ka-ching. And puh-leeze don't tell me that can't be possible because Matthew is so deeply, truly in love with Hannah Lane, as in 'She Jane.' He's British. He's an actor. Hello, they are *all* switch-hitters."

"Hang on a sec, I want to write this down."

She swatted me again. "I'm giving you the goods here, cutie."

"Does Hannah know?"

"Poor thing hasn't a clue. Hannah has the approximate I.Q.

of a parakeet. She's also incredibly naïve. So's Matthew, for that matter, but Henderson loves him the baby boys. In fact, if you don't watch out he'll hit on *you*."

"When?"

"Right now. He just walked in the door. And he's not alone."

In fact, the ex-director of *Wuthering Heights* was accompanied by none other than Matthew and Hannah—not to mention the two-dozen yammering paparazzi who were crowded outside the bistro's glass door like brain-eating zombies.

"What's Henderson doing out in public with them?"

"Poking Morrie in the eye with a sharp stick. What do you think?"

I thought Matthew and Hannah looked incredibly young, which they were. He was twenty-three, she was twenty-two. Also shockingly tiny. They were like a matched pair of miniature movie star dolls. Hannah had huge, protruding green eyes that were set freakishly wide apart, plump, bee-stung lips and flawless ivory skin. Her trademark strawberry blonde ringlets fell practically to her waist. She wore a gauzy off-the-shoulder top that accentuated her fine-boned delicacy, a pair of leggings and flip-flops. Matthew had the jaw and shoulders of a big brute even though he was no more than a junior welterweight, tops. Actually, I thought his jutting jaw and prominent brow made him look like a caveman. But I'm told that women go weak in the knees for cavemen. Matthew's jaw muscles were tightly clenched and he was glowering. Glowering was his thing. He was unshaven and his long, dark brown hair was uncombed. He had on a white T-shirt with the sleeves chopped off to show off his arms, khakis with the cuffs rolled up and a pair of rope-soled espadrilles.

The maître d' greeted them warmly. They started their way past us toward the dining room, Henderson bringing up the rear.

Cricket hurled herself in front of them. "How's the ankle doing, Hannah?"

"My ankle feels perfectly fine," Hannah responded in her trademark soft, trembly voice. "The doctor has cleared me to resume normal activities. I'm back in the dance studio." She almost seemed to be reciting the words, as if they'd been scripted for her.

"That's great, hon. Hey, Matthew, does the name R. J. Farnell mean anything to you?"

"No, it does not," he answered in a haughty, dismissive voice. "Should it?"

"Just wondered if you knew him." Cricket stepped aside so they could pass.

"I thought we were going to keep his name between us," I growled at her.

"Matthew's a Brit. R.J.'s a Brit. I took a shot. Don't look at me that way. This is what I do."

"Do *not* repeat that name again, Cricket."

"Okay, okay. Don't be such a lame-o."

Henderson Lebow was way more anxious for face time with Cricket than the young stars had been. He even seemed happy to see her. "How are you this evening, you little firecracker?"

"I'm making it happen, Henderson. You know Benji Golden?"

The Tony Award-winning director eyed me up and down greedily. He didn't lick his chops like the Big Bad Wolf but he did appear to drool slightly. Henderson was in his fifties but looked younger. He was extremely fit. His tanned face was smooth and unlined, his glossy black hair thick and free of gray. He wore a snug-fitting lime-green Izod shirt with the collar turned up just so and even snugger-fitting blue jeans. "Why, yes, I believe so," he said to me warmly. "I auditioned you for *Bye Bye Birdie*, didn't I?"

"No, sir, you didn't."

"Yet I'm positive we've met."

"You spoke to my drama class at NYU. I asked you a question afterward."

"What did you . . . ?"

"If you thought that the musical comedy was dead."

"And what did I . . . ?"

"You said, 'Not as long as there are people out there who yearn to be swept away to somewhere magical.' "

Henderson arched an eyebrow at me. "God, I'm full of shit. So you're an actor?"

"Private investigator."

"You're kidding."

"He's working for Morrie," Cricket said. "Although he won't admit it."

"Well, good luck with that, Benji. I wish Morrie well. Would you like to know why?"

"Yes, sir, I would."

"Because as long as Morrie's around people won't think *I'm* the biggest scumbag in town." He winked at me, then went off to join Matthew and Hannah, who were seated at a table for four being stared at by everyone in the place.

I went back to work on my cheeseburger while Cricket

thumbed out a quick tweet about what had just transpired. She was never off the clock. "I don't get it," I said to her. "Henderson Lebow can, and apparently does, sleep with any hunky young actor he wants. Why on earth would he sleep with Morrie?"

"Because he's consumed by self-loathing," she answered with great confidence. "Deep down inside, all gay men are."

"Hang on, I want to write this one down, too."

"You didn't used to be so sarcastic, cutie."

"And you didn't used to talk out of your ass."

"It's the Web site," she conceded. "I spew and spew and no one ever tells me to shut up. Plus the *Times* Styles section just called me one of the five most influential people on Broadway. That sort of thing can go to a person's head, believe me."

"Oh, I do."

"OMG!" Cricket gasped, swatting me yet again. My arms used to be black and blue when we were together. She was staring at the front door in wide-eyed disbelief. "OMG!"

The single most powerful and enigmatic man in the entire entertainment industry, Ira Gottfried, the bicoastal chief of Panorama Studios, had just walked in. Ira Gottfried had bankrolled and reaped billions from the Tarzan trilogy. And he had Mathew and Hannah under contract to star in a fourth Tarzan blockbuster. He was a new-age mogul—an ascetic, forty-something tai chi master and practicing Buddhist, a loner with no wife, no kids and no vices. He had no social or romantic life that anyone knew about. Fasted at an ashram in the Mojave Desert for a week at a time to clarify his thoughts. And was famously reserved and understated. He was tall and gaunt. Wore his graying hair in a ponytail. Was dressed in a black silk shirt, black jeans and black suede Puma Classics. He always wore black. I'm guessing his underwear was black, too, though it wasn't something I wanted to devote a lot of time to thinking about. Morrie Frankel had called him Count Dracula. To most people he was known as the Man in Black.

Cricket, who did not lack for balls, barged on over and intercepted him before the maître d' could. "Please tell me this isn't a coincidence, Ira."

"I'm meeting friends for dinner," he said to her quietly, his thin-lipped mouth barely moving. "Don't make it into anything more."

The maître d' led him to his table—the very table that Henderson was sharing with Matthew and Hannah. Cricket followed him like a pesky terrier and, as soon as he sat down, snapped a picture of the power foursome with her camera phone. The maître d' clucked at her and shooed her away, but she was already posting the photo on her Web site by the time she returned to me at the bar.

"They knew you'd do that," I observed.

"Of course they knew," she said, thumbing out a caption to go with the photo. "And they want Morrie to know. You're witnessing history here tonight. The great Morrie Frankel is getting royally hosed. Is this exciting or what?"

I looked over at the four of them. They didn't exactly seem to be hatching a nefarious plot. Just chatting together politely. "What do you suppose they're talking about?"

"I'd say Ira's inviting Henderson to step back in and direct *Wuthering Heights* as soon as Morrie goes under. Which won't be long now."

"Meaning Panorama will bankroll the show?"

"Ira's wanted to bankroll it all along. Matthew and Hannah are his biggest stars, and *Wuthering Heights* has major, major movie upside. But I hear that Morrie won't even return his phone calls. Can you imagine?"

"Do you really think that's what they're talking about?"

She batted her eyelashes at me. "It better be. That's what I just posted."

"Cricket, that's outright speculation."

"That's how I roll. And I happen to be right ninety percent of the time, which gives me a much higher batting average than the so-called responsible mainstream media."

I finished off the last of my cheeseburger, washing it down with a gulp of milk. "I have a serious question for you."

"Fire away, cutie."

"Why is *Wuthering Heights* in so much trouble? I know Hannah broke her ankle, but a cloud's been hanging over this show since Day One. What's the real story?"

Cricket hesitated. "You didn't hear this from me, okay?"

"Okay . . ."

"Matthew and Hannah have been taking voice lessons. And Hannah's singing voice is getting stronger. But Matthew's? Not so much."

"How bad is it?"

"Laugh-out-loud bad. When he breaks into 'You're Still My

Queen' I'm told he sounds shockingly like one of Alvin and the Chipmunks."

"Which one—Alvin, Simon or Theodore?"

She let out a snort. "Does it matter?"

"Oh, it totally does."

"Matthew simply can't pull off a live Broadway performance. The only way *Wuthering Heights* can possibly be staged with Hannah and him headlining it is if somebody else sings Matthew's songs for him and Matthew lip-synchs them. Which Morrie flat out refuses to do. Morrie may be a consummate fucktard but he's a Broadway purist. And I'm with him on this one. Can you *imagine* the blowback if there was a Milli Vanilli meltdown in the middle of a major Broadway musical production? It's too horrifying to even contemplate. But Henderson's okay with the idea. He thinks he can pull it off."

"How do you know this?"

"My boy Bobby is tight with Henderson's personal trainer, and he heard Henderson and Morrie screaming at each other about it one day in Henderson's apartment. This was before Morrie fired Henderson for the penile-related matter."

"Lip-synching," I said disgustedly. "I can't believe that Broadway has fallen this far. Ethel Merman must be spinning in her grave."

"You really, really need to get over your Ethel Merman thing, cutie. This is why you never get laid."

"I get laid."

"Oh, really? When was the last time?"

I peered at her curiously. "Why haven't you broken this story?"

"What story?"

"That Matthew can't sing. That they're between a crag and a hard place."

"Good line. Can I steal it?"

"It's yours. Why haven't you?"

Cricket drank down the last of her Irish coffee, swiping at her mouth with the back of her hand. "Because I don't want to see two hundred people thrown out of work. A lot of folks think I'm a heartless little bitch. But I happen to love the theater. And those people are my friends—the kids in the chorus, the set dressers, lighting guys, ushers, all of them. If *Wuthering Heights* goes under then they're out on the street."

"And what about the other big shows on Broadway?"

"What about them?"

"They have producers of their own, ruthless bastards one and all. Is there any chance those producers dangled R. J. Farnell in front of Morrie—flat out duped him—because they don't want *Wuthering Heights* to open?"

"No way. A hit show is good for everyone. If the public comes to see one show they'll stay to see another. Every producer knows that. Besides, those greedy bastards can barely have a cup of coffee together, let alone conspire to scam somebody as shrewd as Morrie Frankel." She studied me curiously. "Tell me the truth, are you getting any pussy at all?"

"Why are you asking?"

"Because I know lots of desperately horny young actresses who deserve to be treated nice for a change. Want me to hook you up with one?"

"I'll think about it."

"No, you won't. You're still hung up on that One True Love fantasy of yours. It's a myth, Benji. This is me talking. Do yourself a favor, will you? Have some fun for a change. Because, guess what, while you're waiting for that One True Love of yours to come along your whole fucking life is passing you by."

CHAPTER THREE

"AVALON" BY ROXY MUSIC, Mom's favorite band, was blasting from her office when I got home. I found her at her desk tapping away on her laptop, a tall gin and tonic within arm's reach. The lights were low. The rackety window air conditioner was cranked up high.

"You're back," I observed, smiling at her from the doorway.

She turned down the music, smiling back at me. "A person can't pull anything over on Mrs. Golden's sharp-eyed son."

"Did you eat dinner?"

"I had a huge salad with Gretchen before I drove back from the Hamptons. That would be Gretchen Van Deusen of the Hoity-Toity Agency. Gretchen is *the* go-to realtor for luxury rental properties in East Hampton, thank you very much. Want Diego to bring you up something? I think Scotty's special tonight was goulash."

"I'm all set. Where's Rita?"

"Having a late supper with Myron. I practically had to kick her out the door. She was so engrossed in your nudie shots of Boso that she lost track of the time."

"Did she get anywhere?"

"Well, she convinced me that they Photoshopped Boso's vay-jay lips. Does that count?"

My cell phone rang. It was Morrie yet again. This time I took his call. "This is Ben Golden. How may I help you?"

"You can return your fucking phone calls, you little putz!" he roared at me. "Do you *know* how many messages I've left you?!"

"Mr. Frankel . . ."

"If I call you it's for a reason!"

"Mr. Frankel . . ."

"*And* I expect you to call me back, hear me? I'm paying you all of this goddamned money and I still haven't heard a goddamned thing from you!"

"Mr. Frankel, we're devoting a hundred percent of our time to your case. We're making excellent progress, but I'm not in a position to report anything yet, okay?"

"No, it's *not* okay! That little twat Cricket O'Shea just posted a photo of *my* stars and *my* ex-director having dinner at Zoot Alors with none other than Count Dracula himself. She said, flat out *declared*, that he's plotting to steal my show out from under me. So you'll forgive me if I'm just a tiny bit upset!"

"Cricket O'Shea has been known to make stuff up. Don't let her throw you."

"I don't like this," he growled. "I don't like *you*."

"I'm sorry to hear that. If you want to hire someone else just say so."

I heard another voice in the background now from his end.

Then heard him grumble something unintelligible before he said, "Leah thinks I should shut up and let you do your job."

"Leah's a smart woman."

"Hey, I don't need you to tell me that."

"Mr. Frankel, I'll talk to you tomorrow, okay?"

"What time?"

"Just as soon as I have something. Good night, Mr. Frankel." I rang off, letting my breath out with a sigh. "That was Mr. Frankel."

"So I gathered." Mom narrowed her eyes at me. "Weren't you and Cricket romantically involved for a while?"

"I guess you could call it that." I fetched a cold bottle of Long Trail IPA from the little fridge in the outer office, opened it and took a long, thirsty gulp before I flopped down on Mom's sofa next to Gus, who curled up in my lap and started purring. "So tell me about Gretchen Van Deusen of the Hoity-Toity Agency."

"She was a skinny blond society bitch in her late forties. Divorced, bitter, could not keep her mouth shut. You'd have loved her, Bunny." Mom reached for her notepad, scanning through it. "The house on Lily Pond Lane belongs to a power couple that's splitting up. He's a big shot at NBC News. She's on-air talent. Or was. Her job went south when the marriage did. She's suing him. He's suing her. It's love in bloom all over. Meanwhile, their snug little cottage is on the market for five point five million. It has seven bedrooms, five baths, a pool, four acres of land and beach access. Confidentially? Gretchen told me they'd take four point nine mil for it. While they wait for the offers to roll in she's renting it out for thirty thousand a month. A Silicon Valley exec has it this month."

"What about last month?"

Mom took a sip of her gin and tonic, sitting back in her chair. "She rented it to a high-flying British hedge funder named R. J. Farnell. Gretchen described him as quite the charmer. And very interested in the theater, it may interest you to know."

"He told her that?"

"He did. Mind you, she only spoke to him on the phone."

"She rented him the place without ever meeting him?"

"He sent his young executive assistant, a Miss Beausoleil, to look the place over. Gretchen met her there. Miss Beausoleil pulled up in a fancy new Porsche wearing a drop-dead Armani linen pants suit and a pair of Manolo Blahniks. Her briefcase was Louis Vuitton. Her scarf was Hermès. Her—"

"Mom, are you running this or giving me a fashion review?"

"Oh, hush. When I showed her Boso's headshot she made her right away, though she did say that Miss Beausoleil wore horn-rimmed glasses. Oliver Peoples, she thought. Although they might have been Barton Perreira, which are almost exactly—"

"Mom . . ."

"Gretchen gave her a full tour of the house. The girl took pictures of every room with her camera phone and e-mailed them to Farnell. He phoned her right away and said he wanted to take it. She put him on the phone with Gretchen and the deal was made on the spot."

I drank down some more of my Long Trail. "How did Farnell pay her?"

"Cash. Boso had the thirty thou in her briefcase, along with an additional ten thou security deposit."

"And Gretchen handed over the keys to a multimillion dollar house just like that?"

"She's been an East Hampton realtor for twelve years. She's dealt with rock stars, pro athletes, super models. As far as she's concerned, this was business as usual."

"What about references, a signed lease agreement . . . ?"

"I'm guessing Boso schmeared her an extra couple of grand to bypass the usual reference check. And it so happens that Farnell did sign a lease agreement. Boso delivered it to him. He signed it and mailed it back to Gretchen. She showed it to me when we got back to her office. I saw the man's signature."

"I wish we had a Xerox of that lease."

"We do," Mom assured me, smiling faintly.

"God, you're good."

"He provided Gretchen with his residential and business addresses here in the city. I stopped off at his apartment building on East 72nd when I got back. There's no R. J. Farnell living there. And the doorman's never heard of him. And his office address in lower Manhattan—39 Broadway, suite 704—is a fake. There's no suite 704 in that building." Mom set her notepad aside and took another sip of her drink. "I asked around on Lily Pond Lane. Talked to the UPS man, the landscapers, pool guys. No one remembers seeing a man living in that house last month. They do remember seeing the girl. Men never forget a girl like that. Especially one who likes to sun herself by the pool in the nude. The gardener next door couldn't believe his eyes. But he only recalls seeing Boso there by herself. I checked with the gourmet grocers and wine shops and so on. No one made any deliveries out there. Miss Beausoleil returned the keys at the end of the month. Gretchen told me the house was in perfect condition, although it wouldn't surprise me at all if that ten thou security deposit ended up in Gretchen's pocket, too. We're all a bit corrupt, you know."

"Who paid the utility bills?"

"They never got switched over to a new account. Gretchen told me they usually aren't for short-term luxury rentals."

"So R. J. Farnell, alleged hedge fund hotshot, tells Morrie he wants to bankroll *Wuthering Heights* to the tune of twelve mil," I said, mulling it over. "Morrie goes out to R.J.'s estate in East Hampton and comes away convinced that R.J. is his lifeline. But it sounds as if R.J., or whoever he really is, rented the place for the sole purpose of using it that one afternoon to scam Morrie. Agreed?"

"Agreed," Mom said, nodding her head.

"This guy is a pro, because Morrie Frankel is no dummy. Crazed and desperate, yes. A sap? No."

"Morrie was already circling the drain on his own," Mom pointed out. "Why not just stand back and let him go down? Why go to so much trouble?"

"To humiliate him," I reflected, drinking down the last of my IPA.

Mom studied me, her brow creasing. "You look tired, Bunny. You should go up to bed. But first give your mother a kiss."

I got up off the couch and gave her a peck on the forehead. "How about you?"

"I'll lock up soon. I just want to finish inputting my notes." She swiveled around to face her laptop again. "Myron hates it that Rita's here day and night. He's making her miserable."

"That's not possible. Dentists named Myron don't make beautiful women miserable."

"If you ask me, Rita was much better off when she was with you."

"She wasn't 'with' me, Mom. We were just two friends helping each other out. Rita needs a nice, normal, age-appropriate guy like Myron."

"The trouble with nice, normal, age-appropriate guys like Myron is that they insist on being put first. And Rita won't put him ahead of her work. She may be forced to choose. You'd better prepare yourself."

I drew in my breath. "You mean we may lose her?"

"That's exactly what I mean."

"We can always find another computer wiz. But we'll never find another Rita."

"No, we won't," she agreed somberly. "Sweet dreams, Bunny."

I climbed the stairs up toward my apartment. When I reached the third floor landing I encountered Mr. Felcher of 3-B pounding on the door of Mrs. Felcher of 3-A. Mr. Felcher, who is well into his eighties, wore a pair of billowy powder-blue boxer shorts and nothing else. The boxers did not exactly smell fresh. Nor did Mr. Felcher, who is squatly built, hairy and unremittingly grouchy. He and his not-so-adoring wife have been living across the hall from each other since the 1970s.

"Open this goddamned door!" he hollered, pounding on it with his fist.

She hollered something back at him through the closed door that sounded vaguely like: "Fuck off, you old fuck!"

"Good evening, Mr. Felcher. How are you doing?"

"What do *you* want?"

"Is there anything I can help you with, sir?"

"I blew a fuse and that bitch won't give me one."

"Want me to get you one?"

"I *want* you to take better care of this damned building. I *never* blew fuses when your father was around."

This was true. But my dad also insisted that the Felchers pay their rent every month, which Mom's too big a softie to do. She thinks it's a sin to dun the elderly.

"Shall I get that fuse for you, Mr. Felcher?"

"Are you still here? Why can't you mind your own damned business!"

"Certainly, sir. I can do that."

Mom's floor-through apartment is one flight up on the fourth floor. Mine's on the top floor, which is freezing cold in the winter, because our furnace is dying, and toasty warm all summer long because, well, heat rises. I also enjoy unlimited access to my own private tar beach—also known as the roof.

I inherited roomfuls of comfy overstuffed furniture from my grandmother's apartment in Flatbush. I swear it still smells like kasha knishes on hot, muggy evenings. The apartment does have cross ventilation, and I keep an assortment of strategically placed fans going day and night. Plus I have a window air conditioner in my bedroom. But I can only use that when I go to bed. If I try to run it while I have lights on anywhere else then I'll blow a fuse just like Mr. Felcher had. Our building is one of the only ones left in the neighborhood that still has fuse boxes instead of circuit breakers, and it's getting to be really hard to find fuses at a hardware store. Really hard to find a hardware store for that matter. There used to be a big one around the corner on Amsterdam that had been in business forever. It's now a bar where hip young professionals go to drink mojitos and play Ping-Pong.

I stripped off my clothes and took a long, cool shower. Flossed carefully after I brushed my teeth because Myron said that if I don't floss regularly my gums will recede and my teeth will fall out. I don't think Myron likes me. I drank two tall glasses of ice water, turned off every light in the place and took my laptop and cell phone with me into my bedroom, which has a big four-poster walnut bed and matching chest of drawers. I flicked on the AC, climbed into bed and lay there in the darkness, fighting to stay awake as the room began to cool. I don't welcome sleep. I never want to sleep.

My cell rang just after midnight. It was Rita. "Did I wake you up?"

"Not a chance. What's going on?"

"Well, I'm in bed with all three of my laptops."

"That doesn't leave much room for Myron."

"Not a problem. He stood me up."

"Rita, you promised me—no details about your sex life."

"Not funny, little lamb. I was on my way to meet him at our favorite Chinese restaurant on Second Avenue. He phoned me and said he couldn't make it due to a 'prior commitment.' "

"Meaning what, he had to perform an emergency root canal?"

"I don't know," Rita sighed. "And that's enough about him, okay? I've been working ever since I got home and I've made serious progress on those Boso shots. Want to hear what I've got?"

"I'm all ears."

"I couldn't find a thing in her black velvet thong gallery. The nightstand's bare, and there are no reflections in the pictures on the wall. But I had much better luck with the yacht. Or I should say sloop. She's a Pearson 365. The Pearson 365 is thirty-six feet long and was built between 1976 and 1982. There are still quite a few of them out there. They go for around fifty thou. I just sent you a link from a yacht broker's Web site. See it?"

"Hang on . . ." I flipped open my laptop and downloaded the link. "Yeah, that sure looks like it."

"I also zoomed in on the shoreline in the background. You were right—it's the South Shore. Babylon Cove to be exact."

"Awesome. This gets me in the game. You're the best, Rita."

"Slow down, because it gets more awesome. I hit a home run with that video of Boso on the balcony—thanks to this killer new image-enhancing software I've got. You were also right about that reflection in her sunglasses. Hang on, I'm sending you the image now. It's digitally magnified and sharpened, okay? And I *think* you're going to recognize a certain something. . . ."

"Hey, that's the Statue of Liberty," I exclaimed, studying the digitally enhanced image on my screen. "And there's Lower Manhattan. And the Verrazano Bridge over there. . . . I give up, where do you get this kind of a view?"

"From a high-rise building on Staten Island. The Rosebank section, to be specific. Thanks to the slight convexity of her sunglass lenses we can see downward. Look at the very bottom of the image. Do you see that greenery just before the water's edge?"

"Yeah. It's a park of some kind."

"It's the Alice Austin House, a National Historic Landmark that's on the corner of Hylan Boulevard and Edgewater Street about two miles from the Staten Island Ferry Terminal. I searched the realty listings for high-rise units around there, and it turns out there's a whole nest of high-rise luxury condos on Hylan Boulevard that I had no idea even existed. Staten Island's not exactly ground zero for chic living, know what I'm saying? I took a virtual tour of a twelfth-floor unit in The Gateway. We're talking uber high-end. Doorman, swimming pool, underground parking, the works. And they're asking a sweet six hundred thou for a measly little one-bedroom. The reason being that every unit enjoys panoramic views of the Statue of Liberty from its floor-to-ceiling windows and private balcony. And guess what? The twelfth floor of The Gateway has almost the same exact view that's reflected in Boso's sunglasses."

"I'm liking the sound of this, Rita."

"Wait, it gets even better. I started checking out the neighboring buildings, okay? Want to guess who owns the Crown Towers right across the street from The Gateway? Top Hat Property Management. Want to guess who owns the controlling interest in Top Hat? Mr. Joe Minetta, boss of the Minetta crime family."

Right away, my wheels were spinning. Morrie was in deep to Joe Minetta, according to Leah Shimmel. Not a surprise if the highly diversified Minetta family happened to be in the highly lucrative Internet porn trade. Also not a surprise if they kept a webcam girl like Boso stashed in an apartment building somewhere off the radar. And it doesn't *get* more off the radar than

Staten Island. Boso was linked to Morrie's missing angel, R. J. Farnell. That much I knew. But what was the link between R. J. Farnell and Joe Minetta? "Rita, does the Crown Towers have a health spa?"

"Um, it has a pool but I don't see anything about a spa. Why?"

"Check out Boso's abs. She works out like a fiend, wouldn't you say?"

"Yes, I would. Pilates, I'd bet."

"Where's the nearest Pilates club?"

"Hang on . . . Okay, there's a Sharp Fitness Center two blocks away on Bay Street. They offer Pilates and yoga."

"You done good, Rita."

"*You* done good. You're the one who noticed that reflection. The moron who shot the video was too busy getting a chubby. She *is* a sexy little thing."

"She's okay," I said quietly.

"Are *you* okay?"

"Why, don't I sound okay?"

"No, you sound lonesome and mournful. Do you want to talk? I'm always here for you, you know."

"I'm fine, Rita. Really."

"Okay, if you say so. Sleep tight, little lamb."

I rang off and watched eighteen-year-old Jonquil Beausoleil of Ruston, Louisiana, rub baby oil on her naked self for a little while until I decided that that was a really bad idea and shut down my laptop. Then I lay there staring at the ceiling in the darkness. Not that it's ever totally dark in the city. There was enough of a glow from the streetlights and neighboring buildings that I could make out the intricate pattern of cracks and water stains in the plaster over my bed. As I studied them I thought about Cricket and wondered why things hadn't worked out between us. Too soon, probably. My scars had still been fresh. I thought about Rita and how much I missed being with her. I thought about calling one of the numbers in my little black book. Except, well, I don't have a little black book. So instead I just lay there, restless and alone.

But I didn't sleep. I don't sleep. Not if I can help it.

That's when the nightmares come.

CHAPTER FOUR

"GOT A DELIVERY for a Miss Bo-so-leel from Rosebank Florists," I announced, standing there in the well-kept lobby of the Crown Towers with the dozen long-stemmed roses that I'd just bought at a shop on Bay Street.

The uniformed doorman gave me the once over. I was wearing a striped T-shirt, reversed Yankees cap, my third-best pair of four-year-old madras shorts from the Gap and a pair of drug store flip-flops. I passed for seventeen. The doorman was a burly guy in his fifties who looked as if he'd put in a solid two decades as a bouncer in a strip club.

"Who's that you say?" he demanded gruffly.

"Miss Bo-so-leel. Or I guess it could be *Mrs.* Bo-so-leel. Am I pronouncing that right?"

"Who do I look like, Alex Trebek?"

"Well, is this the right building?"

"I'll make sure she gets them."

"But *I'm* supposed to make sure gets them."

"You just did, Skippy."

"She's supposed to sign for them, I mean."

He scribbled his signature across my delivery slip. "Now beat it."

I beat it. Strolled a hundred yards down Hylan Boulevard and across the street to my dad's Caddie. It's a '92 burgundy Brougham with a white vinyl top and matching burgundy leather interior. The Brougham had been his pride and joy. These days it's our company car. I got in, rolled down the windows and took off the Yankee cap and striped T-shirt. I wore a plain white T-shirt underneath. It was Day Four of the Heat Wave of the Century. Supposed to top out at 103 in Central Park that afternoon. Possibly be a degree or two cooler out on Staten Island. Hylan was quiet on a weekday morning. Everyone had gone to work, or so it seemed. A plumbing company van was parked two doors down from the Crown Towers. Not many other cars were parked there.

I settled in for a long wait. Stakeouts can be downright tedious. I have no idea how long I'm going to be sitting there. So I bring a patient attitude and a ton of supplies. I had my iPod loaded with dozens of my favorite Broadway musicals. I had my laptop, all three New York newspapers and director Elia Kazan's incredibly candid memoir. I love to read showbiz memoirs, the juicier the better. I had my Nikon D80 with a zoom lens. I had three pairs of sunglasses, a half-dozen baseball caps and a stack of T-shirts in assorted colors. I had a cooler filled with sandwiches from Scotty's and a dozen bottles of water, since it's super important to stay hydrated when you're sitting in a parked car on a hot summer day. I had an empty gallon jug, since it's also super important to have something to pee into while you're staying hydrated. I had a toilet kit, a blanket and a pillow. I was prepared to live in that car all day and night if I had to.

My Smith & Wesson Chief's Special was locked in the glove compartment, fully loaded in case I needed it. And I have.

I waited. No one came or went through the front door of the Crown Towers except for the mailman, who had one of those rolling carts that they use. A black Land Rover took off from the underground parking garage. I couldn't see who was driving it. The windows were tinted. I waited. Had one ham and cheese sandwich, two bottles of water and waited some more, surprised that Morrie hadn't called me yet to scream at me some more. Possibly his head had exploded.

I'd been waiting there for about two hours when a beat-up Chevy Impala pulled up behind me and parked. A woman got out from behind the wheel, came around to the Brougham's passenger door and got in next to me. She was a Latina in her mid-thirties with large, liquid dark eyes and shiny black hair. She wore slacks and a sleeveless cotton blouse.

"How are you this morning, Mr. Golden?" she asked, her voice brusque and officious.

"A tad warm but otherwise fine. And you are . . . ?"

"Sue Herrera. I'm a detective with OCCB." OCCB is the NYPD's Organized Crime Control Bureau. "It so happens that we have the Crown Towers under surveillance, Mr. Golden."

"The plumbing van, am I right?"

"My boys ran your plate. As soon as your name came up I called Legs. He told me you're good people. He *didn't* tell me that you and your cute widdle nose just popped out of a Disney cartoon." She looked at me in amusement. "How old are you anyhow?"

"Excuse me a sec." I speed dialed Detective Lieutenant Larry

Diamond, better known as Legs because he hates, hates the name Larry. Legs is the top homicide detective in New York City. My dad was his rabbi. He's like a big brother to me.

When he picked up, I said, "I'm sitting here on the Island of Staten with a Herrera comma Sue."

"Yeah, I was kind of expecting that. She'll bust your balls but she won't burn you. Only, listen up, when she asks you if you're available say no. Don't go there, little dude."

"Why not?"

"Just don't."

"Whatever you say, Legs." I rang off.

"What did he say?" Sue Herrera asked me, her gaze softening. Legs has that effect on most women.

"That I can trust you."

"He told me he's been trying to get you on the job for two years."

"That was my father's life, not mine."

"We need to have a conversation, Mr. Golden."

"About what? And make it Benji, will you?"

"What do you want with Jonquil Beausoleil, Benji?"

"Sorry, Jonquil who?"

She heaved a sigh of annoyance. "Don't play dumb. We've flipped the doorman. He passed the word to the mailman, who's one of ours, that you tried to deliver flowers to her. And now you're staked out here."

"I just really like Staten Island."

"And I really *don't* like having my chain jerked. You need to move along, Benji. You might set off alarm bells."

"I wouldn't worry about that. No one ever mistakes me for

the law. If anything, I'm a welcome distraction from that dumb-assed plumbing van of yours. Wow, talk about obvious."

"We change vans every day," she said defensively.

"And the two of us sitting here talking like this? Not exactly my idea of subtle either."

She shifted in her seat, looking deeply into my eyes for a moment. Then she slapped me across the face. Hard.

"What'd you do that for?" I demanded.

"If anyone in the Crown Towers is watching us they'll think we're having a lovers' quarrel. Besides, the boys in the van needed a good laugh."

My cheek stung like hell but I refused to rub it. Wouldn't give her the satisfaction. "You're not very nice, are you, Sue Herrera?"

"I'm not paid to be nice. Neither are you." She looked at me some more, tilting her head slightly. "You have old eyes. Anyone ever tell you that? Richie, my ex, looked like a grown man but on the inside he was still a boy. You look like a boy yet your eyes tell me you're a man. *How* old are you?"

"Old enough to not get chased off a paying case by a chesty detective from OCCB."

"Did you just call me chesty?"

"Would you prefer busty?"

"I'd prefer you to get the hell out of here."

"I thought we needed to have a conversation."

"You're interested in a webcam girl named Jonquil Beausoleil. Why?"

"The usual reason."

"She's a runaway?"

I nodded. "From Ruston, Louisiana. Was supposed to start

college this fall. Instead, she dropped out of high school and made her way up here in search of fame and fortune."

"Her parents hire you to find her?"

"Your turn. Why's OCCB staking out the Crown Towers? I'm aware that Joe Minetta owns it. What's going on here that you're so interested in?"

"That's need to know, Benji."

"As in I don't?"

"As in correct."

"As in I don't think we can do business, Sue Herrera."

"Legs didn't tell me you were a stubborn pain."

"I'm just trying to do an honest day's work."

She sat there in silence for a moment. "Okay, here's what worries me. Let's say you talk to her. What if she tips them off?"

"Tips them off about what?"

She didn't respond. Just stared at me.

"Sorry, Sue Herrera. I still don't think we can do business."

"Listen, Benji, you can't just whisk this girl off to La Guardia and put her on the next flight to NOLA. Her hands are dirty. Hers and the others—Luze, Sonya, Little Mutt . . ."

" 'Little Mutt'?"

"The only way that Jonquil Beausoleil's going home is if she cooperates with our investigation. If you can convince her to do that then *maybe* I can help you out. What do you say?"

"I say, nice talking to you, Sue Herrera."

"Fine, have it your way. But if you mess up my thing you will be on my bad side. And you won't like that, Benji." She reached over and gave my cheek a gentle pat. I didn't flinch one bit. I want some credit for that. Then she got out, climbed back in her sedan and drove away.

Thirty minutes later Jonquil Beausoleil came bounding out the front door of the Crown Towers with a nylon gym bag thrown over one shoulder and started her way down the block, her stride brisk and athletic. She wore a yellow tank top cropped above her navel, blue spandex shorts and running shoes. Her long, shimmering blond hair was gathered in a ponytail.

I waited until she'd turned the corner onto Bay Street before I started up the Brougham and went after her. There was a diner on the corner. A deli, a Chinese take-out place. I pulled up alongside of her with the window rolled down and called out, "Boso, my name's Benji Golden. We need to talk."

She kept right on walking, ignoring me.

"I'm not a stalker creep. I work for Morrie Frankel. He sent me, okay?"

She stopped, looking at me in surprise. "Why would he do that?" Her Southern accent was faint but definitely there.

"Because he's in trouble. Please get in."

She stayed put on the sidewalk in the broiling heat. "*Who* are you?"

"Benji Golden. I'm a private investigator. Morrie hired me to find you."

"What for? Why didn't he just call me? I *gave* him my new cell number."

"He has your cell number?"

"Well, yeah."

"Okay, I don't understand."

"That makes two of us. Are you playing me?"

"I'm not playing you. I'm a licensed private investigator. You have absolutely no reason to fear me. Please get in. We need to talk. It's important."

Boso scrunched her mouth over to one side like a teenager, which was exactly what she was. "I don't like this."

"I don't blame you, but you can trust me. I'm on your side."

"No one's on my side."

"Get in, please?"

She took a hesitant step toward me. "You swear you're for real?"

"I swear."

She got in, smelling of cool minty toothpaste and warm sweaty girl. She wasn't wearing any makeup or lipstick. Up close and in person she looked even younger and smaller than she had on my computer screen. Also considerably more ordinary. She was no Hannah Lane. Her complexion wasn't perfect. Her features weren't exquisitely sculpted. Her chin, in particular, had a stubborn thrust to it. Jonquil Beausoleil looked exactly like who she'd been up until a few months ago—a pretty, blue-eyed, blond cheerleader. And I still didn't like what I saw in those blue eyes.

"How'd you find me?" she wanted to know.

"It's what I do." I eased the Brougham down Bay Street, which was badly potholed and patched. The City doesn't take very good care of the streets on Staten Island. Or anything else. I drove past her Sharp Fitness Center, which was just past Clifton Avenue next to Tony's Brick Oven Pizza, and kept on going. "Why did Morrie hire me if he knows how to reach you?"

Boso gazed at me cautiously. "You tell me. What'd he say?"

"He said that R. J. Farnell is his last best hope for saving *Wuthering Heights*, that Farnell has vanished and that you're the only one who'll know where he is. I know that it was you who rented the house on Lily Pond Lane. I know that the home and office addresses Farnell gave the realtor were bogus. And that his hedge fund is bogus. So who is he and what the hell's going on?"

"Wow, how can anybody be so smart and so dumb at the same time?"

"What does that mean?"

"It means you don't know a *thing*," she said, shaking her blond head.

As I drove by the imposing brick tower of the Church of St. Mary I noticed in my rearview mirror that we had company. An unmarked sedan with two beefy guys in it was staying a careful two cars back. "Oh, hell, why would she go and do that? Where is the trust? Where is the love?"

"You talk funny." Boso peered at me from across the seat. "And you look kind of twerpy to be a detective, if you don't mind me saying."

"I don't mind. Farmer John says hi, by the way."

She blinked at me in astonishment. "How is he?"

"He misses you. So does Leon."

"Who's Leon?"

"The kitten."

"Oh, right . . ."

"John's in love with you, in case you're interested."

"I'm not. I'm over him."

"Totally understandable. He's tall, handsome, rich, compassionate. Hell, the guy's nothing but bad news."

"He's a nice guy, but I couldn't love him back. I'm just all about my career right now. That's why I left. Did he . . . does he know what I'm doing for work?"

"Nope. Neither does your mother." I glanced over at her. "Or your stepfather."

She stiffened instantly, her jaw tightening.

"How old were you when he started in on you? Fifteen, sixteen? Let me guess—he told you that if you said one word to your mother about it he'd claim *you* seduced *him* and you were an evil nympho slut who ought to be locked away somewhere."

All of the color had drained from her face. "I—I don't know what you mean." Her voice was a hollow whisper.

"Yeah, you do. You don't have to pretend with me. I saw it in your eyes the first time Morrie showed me your photo. You can see it in my eyes, too, if you care to look closely enough. People like us, we recognize each other."

"People like us?"

"I'm a rape victim, too."

She began to breathe rapidly in and out, gulping. "Could you . . . please pull over?"

I pulled over to the curb. Our tail pulled over, too. Boso jumped out and threw up her breakfast. She stayed there a moment, doubled over, gasping. Then she got back in, her eyes avoiding mine.

"You want something to drink?" I offered. "A breath mint? A premoistened antibacterial towelette?"

"What are you, a rolling mini-mart?"

"I like to be prepared." I steered us back into the flow of traffic, our tail joining us.

She turned around to check out my supplies in the backseat. "Is that a jug of apple juice on the floor?"

"Not exactly."

"Okay, eeeeeeew."

"There's water in the cooler."

She grabbed herself a bottle and took a long drink.

"Feel better now?"

"I'm okay. I must have eaten some bad clams last night."

"Try again. You're a vegan. And don't bullshit me. Don't even try. I can see right through you." We came to a stop at a red light at Willow Avenue, where there was a gas station and not much else. "I need for you to hang on, okay? I'm going to shake our tail."

"Someone's *tailing* us? Oh, this is just great."

"You may want to close your eyes."

No sane cop is willing to risk life and limb on a routine tail job. That makes it pretty easy to lose a police tail. You just have to do something incredibly reckless and foolhardy. Like, say, make an illegal left turn from the right lane across an intersection of oncoming traffic while a dozen furious drivers are honking and waving their fists at you and the blonde riding next to you is screaming her head off.

"I *told* you to close your eyes," I reminded her as I floored it down Willow and took the first quick left onto Langere Place. Then I made a screeching left onto Lynhurst Avenue, a right onto Anderson Street and circled my way back to Bay Street by way of St. Mary's Avenue. I took that back to Hylan Boulevard and then shot way onto the Staten Island Expressway.

"Hey, wait, where are you taking me?" Boso protested.

"I'll bring you right back. I'm not kidnapping you. We're members of the same club, remember?"

Boso shifted the gym bag at her feet and stared out the window at the traffic on the expressway, scrunching her mouth to one side again.

"Want to talk about it?"

"There's nothing to talk about," she said woodenly. "He did whatever he wanted to me because he could. My mom wouldn't believe me when I told her. Didn't want to. She thought I blamed him for what happened to my dad. So as soon as I saved enough money I left. That chapter of my life is over now."

"No, it's not. It'll never be over. That's our curse."

She looked at me curiously. "Was it a priest who did it to you?"

"I'm Jewish."

"So, like, it was a rabbi?"

I shook my head. "I ran away to Hollywood three weeks before I graduated from high school. When I was down to my last twenty-three cents a real nice guy named Larry offered to buy me a meal. Then he introduced me to his friend Steve. Next thing I knew they were both doing whatever they wanted to me in a motel room. My dad found me there three days later, drugged and dehydrated."

"How on earth did he find you?"

"He was the best detective on the NYPD."

"What is he now?"

"Dead."

"Do you . . . ?"

"Do I what?"

"Get nightmares?"

I nodded. "All the time."

"Me, too. I hate going to sleep. If I could just function twenty-four hours a day without sleep I'd be so much happier."

"Me, too."

"How about . . . sex? With someone who you like, I mean."

"That takes time, but I'm getting there. You?"

"Whenever John touched me I'd cringe and get all tense. I *couldn't* tell him why. I just told him I've always been shy and I—I . . ." She trailed off, breathing in and out. "I don't usually talk about this."

"I don't either."

"I mean, we hardly even know each other, Bingo."

"It's Benji."

"Oh, right. Sorry."

We were on the Verrazano Bridge now heading over the Narrows toward Brooklyn. Off in the distance, the lower Manhattan skyline was shrouded in a cloud of steamy, putrid smog.

"Talk to me about R. J. Farnell."

"Are you *sure* you're not playing me?"

"Why would I want to do that?"

"People do all sorts of things for weird reasons."

"I'm not playing you. What you see is what you get. You told me I don't know anything. What don't I know?"

Boso took a sip of water and gazed out at the skyline for a moment. "Well, just for starters, there is no such person as R. J. Farnell."

CHAPTER FIVE

"THERE'S NO R. J. FARNELL?"

"There's no R. J. Farnell."

"Okay, maybe we'd better start from the beginning."

"Ya think?" Boso chided me, shaking her blond head. "Listen, meeting Morrie's the first big break I've gotten since I came to New York, okay? I mean, he's like a major, major producer. And he promised he'd put me in *Wuthering Heights*, okay? Hire me as the understudy for Isabella, Edgar's sister. If I'd do a sort of favor for him."

We'd crossed over the bridge into the Bay Ridge section of Brooklyn by now and were cruising the Gowanus Expressway.

"What kind of a favor?"

"He told me he was playing an elaborate prank on a friend, which is something that rich New York guys do, I guess. What do I know? I'm just a little girl from Dumbfuckistan. And, let me tell you, when that man phoned me up I was *so* excited. All I've ever wanted to be my whole life is an actress. Except for when I thought about being a massage therapist. And don't laugh. Not the sleazy kind. I mean somebody who helps people with chronic pain. I think anatomy's real interesting. Did you know that giraffes and mice have the same exact number of bones in their necks? Nineteen. Guess how many we have. Go on, guess."

"I really have no idea. How did Morrie—?"

"Seven."

"How did he get your phone number?"

"I auditioned for a role in the chorus. Me and everyone else. There were people lined up all the way around the block."

"A cattle call, sure. Been there, done that."

"Wait, you're an *actor*?"

"I was. Did a couple of episodes of *Law & Order*, a week on a soap."

Boso looked at me in astonishment. "Who *are* you, my brother from another mother?"

"You'd like my mother, actually. She used to be a pole dancer."

"What happened to your acting career?"

"The phone stopped ringing. And my family's business needed me."

"Don't you miss it? You must."

"We were talking about you, remember?"

"Right, okay. No need to get touchy, Mr. Sensitive." She gazed back out the window. "I couldn't believe it when my cell rang and it was Morrie Frankel on the other end."

"Did you leave your headshot there after the cattle call?"

"Yeah, I did. And he told me an associate of his had recommended me."

"Was it Vicki Arduino?"

"He didn't say."

"What was the favor Morrie asked you to do?"

"Pretend to be this guy Farnell's executive assistant. Drive out to East Hampton and rent a fancy house for a month. He gave me an outfit to wear and the keys to a killer Porsche. Plus a briefcase stuffed with cash. It was kind of fun, actually. I got to act all bitchy with the realtor. Plus Morrie let me housesit out there. I swam in the pool and worked on my all-over tan, which I need for my modeling. A real tan is so much better than a salon tan. When you know it's real you *project* that it's real."

"The realtor has a signed lease agreement. Who signed it?"

"Morrie did. He talked to her on the phone, too, British accent and all."

"Did he ever show up out there?"

"Yeah, he came out once, on a Saturday, and took me to lunch at this super-fancy place in Sag Harbor called the American Hotel. A whole bunch of people kept coming over to our table and saying hi to him. Don't ask me who any of them were. They all seemed rich and super impressed with themselves."

"Did they ask Morrie what he was doing out there?"

"They did. He said he was visiting a new backer. Me they ignored. I was just there to look nice. I had the seasonal mixed greens, which turned out to be arugula drowning in citrus-herbal vinaigrette. Morrie had clams and a steak and huge piece of strawberry shortcake. He sprays food when he talks. He's a really disgusting eater."

Not to mention a major league bullshit artist. The great Morrie Frankel was paying us good money to find someone who he was fully aware didn't exist—because he'd made him up. What in the hell for? "Tell me about that phony Web site for the Venusian Society. Did Morrie set that up himself?"

"Not even. He isn't tech savvy."

"Is Leah?"

"Who's Leah?"

"His assistant."

"I wouldn't know. I've never dealt with her. Just Morrie. And he . . ." Boso suddenly let out a gasp, her eyes widening as she stared out the windshield ahead of us. "Oh, lord . . ."

We were descending into the Brooklyn-Battery Tunnel, which burrows its way under the East River into lower Manhattan. She didn't speak the whole time we were down in the tunnel. Or breathe, near as I could tell. Just sat there rigid with her fists clenched until we emerged back into bright daylight amongst the impossibly tall towers of the financial district.

"Are you okay?"

"I *hate* tunnels," she gasped, inhaling deeply. "I always think they're about to cave in right on top of me."

"How are you with the subway?"

"*Hate* it. I need to be in the fresh air and sunshine. Hey, listen, I don't mean to be rude but where are you taking me?"

"Not to worry. You're in safe hands." I steered us uptown on West Street, skirting alongside of the Hudson River toward TriBeCa and the West Village. "So who set up that phony Web site?"

"Petey. He's the webmaster for *sweetgirls* and *babesalone*. He works downstairs in the computer room."

"You mean at the Crown Towers?"

"Yeah. He's very shy, but a total wiz. Pretty much the brains of the outfit. Although don't let his cousin, Little Joe, hear you say that. Little Joe thinks *he* runs things."

"Are you talking about Joe Minetta, Jr.?"

"Yeah. He thinks he's some kind of rock star because his dad owns the company."

West Street becomes Eleventh Avenue once you hit Gansevoort in the West Village. I took that uptown past the Chelsea Piers—home to Silver Screen Studios, where I filmed my guest shots on *Law & Order* and also auditioned for a Mucinex commercial that I didn't get.

"By 'the company' you mean the Minetta crime family. You do know that you're working for the mob, don't you?"

"You make them sound like bad people."

"They *are* bad people."

"No, you're wrong. The guys I work for are, like, total sweeties. They went to Seton Hall together. They're frat boys. And the girls are real nice, too."

I took Twelfth Avenue past the Javits Center and Hell's Kitchen, or Clinton as people now prefer to call it. When we reached Midtown I hung a right onto West 57th and maneuvered us toward Lincoln Center, where I ditched the Brougham in one of those garages that charge by the half hour. Morrie Frankel was still paying for my time. And, for all I knew, Sue Herrera had put out a BOLO on me. She seemed like the vindictive type.

"Let's walk," I said.

Boso wouldn't budge. "*Where* are you taking me?"

I grabbed us two water bottles from the cooler in back, then reached for her gym bag on the floor at her feet. There was something inside of it that was surprisingly heavy and clunky. "Here, you may want this," I said, placing the bag in her lap.

"Why should I go anywhere with you?" she demanded.

"I've been sitting in this car for hours. I think better when I stretch my legs."

"What's there to think about?"

"How we're going to get you out of this mess that you're in."

"I'm not in any mess."

"Trust me, you are. So just shut up and walk with me, okay?"

She shut up and walked with me. She was at least two inches shorter than I am. Maybe even three. It felt kind of nice to walk with a girl who didn't tower over me. We headed west on West 66th Street. After one block Boso no longer had to wonder where we were going—we'd run smack into Central Park, which was crowded with people seeking relief from the heat. There was deep shade and coolness to be found in the park. Young mothers were out pushing their double-wide all-terrain strollers. Vendors were selling cold drinks and Italian ices. I steered us toward the Sheep's Meadow. Every guy who walked in our direction eyeballed Boso as he went by. She was eye candy. A tanned, toned blonde in a cropped, skin-tight tank top and spandex shorts. She seemed oblivious to their stares. The male of the species, I supposed, had been staring at her for as long as she could remember.

"I'm not in any mess," she said to me with great insistence, her gym bag thrown over one shoulder. "So I'm a webcam girl. So I take my clothes off. Maybe that seems sleazy to you or whatever. But to me it's just an acting gig."

I led her in the direction of the Mall. When we reached the Bandshell she came to a halt, her jaw stuck out. "Hey, wait, this is where I met . . ."

"Farmer John. I know."

"I'm not going back to him."

"What *are* you going to do? Because you can't go back to the Crown Towers."

"You promised you weren't kidnapping me."

"I'm not. I'll take you back there if that's what you really want. But you're not safe there, trust me."

"Why should I?" she demanded.

"Because I have no reason to lie to you." I resumed walking. Grudgingly, she tagged along. "How did you end up there anyhow?"

"I answered an ad. Went to an office on Canal Street where some middle-aged woman took a bunch of photos of me. Next day she called me back and I went to a studio on East 36th Street, where I did some swimsuit shots with a photographer who said he'd shot spreads for *Paris Vogue* and was in contact with the top modeling agencies. His name was Gunnar and he had this serious German accent. Told me he was always on the lookout for girls to model for, like, Vicky's Secret and the *Sports Illustrated* Swimsuit Edition. He said I was very natural and all-American."

"Did he pay you?"

"No, but he didn't charge me either. And that's epic. After I left John I crashed in Cobble Hill with a girl I knew from an acting workshop. That's where I was when Gunnar called me to do another shoot. This time I met him at an apartment on East 64th Street. He said he wanted me on a bed wearing a black velvet thong and nothing else, but that I'd be lying on my stomach so you wouldn't be able to see my boobs."

"This would be the Cassia gallery that's on *sweetgirls*."

"You saw it?" She glanced at me shyly. "I was okay with it

once I relaxed. Gunnar made it all seem fun. Not slutty or whatever. Just kind of flirty. And there's nothing you can't see in any slick fashion magazine. He seemed real pleased. Told me he'd show the photos to some people he knew at a modeling agency."

We'd reached the Bethesda Fountain and the Rowboat Lake. Strolled our way around the lake in the direction of the 72nd Street Boathouse.

"And then what happened?"

"Gunnar wanted to shoot me on a yacht *and* pay me a thousand bucks for the day. Me and this Puerto Rican girl named Luze. She also goes by Tamaya and Angelique. So we drove out to, like, a yacht club on Long Island. These two guys were waiting there for us to sail the thing. They were pretty skeevy looking. I was glad Luze was along. I wouldn't have gone out with them if I was by myself. I'm not that stupid. Gunnar shot Luze and me together at first, sunning ourselves on deck with our bikinis on. When he asked us to lose our bikinis I was okay with it. So was Luze. He had us hold hands like little girls. It was totally innocent, and real artistic. And then he shot me by myself. He wanted to see some of my gymnastics moves. I'm pretty flexible."

"You're *very* flexible."

"I've worked real hard to be in the kind of shape I am. So I figured, hey, if someone wants to pay me for it what's the harm, right? Luze was right there cheering me on. It was *fun*. And you want to know what I was thinking the whole time Gunnar was shooting me? I was thinking about my mother's dirty, creepy asshole of a husband. How he'd be drooling over me and wanting me but can't have me. Not anymore. Not ever. And that felt good in a weird sort of way." She shot a worried look at me. "Does that sound crazy?"

"Not to me."

"Gunnar placed both of my galleries on the Web sites. And they liked me so much they wanted to make me a webcam girl just like Luze. So I moved in across the hall from her in this big, beautiful apartment in the Crown Towers with a killer view of the Statue of Liberty. I mean, it's *gorgeous*. And Luze is real sweet. She's from Camden, New Jersey, and used to be in this real abusive relationship with a gangbanger. She's much better off now."

"How many girls are living there?"

"There's four of us to a floor. And we have the top four floors. That makes sixteen, right? We're in and out of each other's places. We have a lot of fun together. Go shopping for clothes and stuff."

"How do you pay for the clothes and stuff?"

"The boys give us credit cards and tell us to go knock yourself out. That's sort of how we get paid."

"Whose credit cards are they?"

She frowned at me. "I don't know what you mean."

"When you use a card does it have your name on it?"

"Does that matter?"

"It matters."

"Well, no, it says I'm little Miss So and So from Wherever, USA. I have a driver's license that says it, too. And then I give it all back and the next time they give me a whole new set of cards with a whole new name."

"And you're okay with that?"

"Why not? I love to shop. We all do. We get to buy whatever

we want. A lot of the time the boys give us lists of things they want us to buy for them, too."

"Like what?"

"All kinds of stuff. Fancy wristwatches, sets of golf clubs, cases of really expensive wine. One of the boys will chauffeur us around from store to store. We have a rockin' good time. They're real nice girls, all except for Little Mutt. She's kind of stuck up."

"Why do they call her Little . . . No, wait, I don't want to know. You said there's a computer room downstairs?"

"Yeah, that's where Petey and the nerd squad hang. A lot of them live in the building, too. But, like I said, they're pretty harmless. And the work's super easy. I just have to hang out and be myself while the webcam follows me around. I do my morning stretches. I make myself a smoothie, take a shower. Big whoop, right? It's good acting experience, actually. I'm getting real comfortable in front of the camera. And they haven't asked me to do anything I'm not comfortable doing."

"Do you do private chats?"

"Well, yeah."

"What about parties?"

"What kind of parties?"

"The kind where a bunch of rich guys sit around and watch naked girls go down on each other."

Boso made a face. "Ugh, no. I'd never do that. I'm an *actress*."

"If you say so."

She glanced at me sharply. "Are you going to give me a lecture now?"

"Nope, I don't do lectures. But I will give you a forecast. Next, they'll want you to do a girl-on-girl video."

"That's just playacting. So what?"

"Then they'll want you to do one with a guy."

"I'm not a porn skank. I won't do that."

"Yeah, you will. Luze will be there to cheer you on again. And you'll end up convincing yourself it really wasn't so bad. The guy was nice enough. And you were just 'performing.' Next you'll take on two guys at once. You'll need to get high to do that. You've got to be sky high to act like it's fun to have two guys use you like a cheap whore."

"That's just disgusting! *You're* disgusting! And you're talking to me like I'm some hick. You don't understand my situation at all."

"Really? So tell me about your situation."

"I'm getting what I want, okay? *That's* my situation. Morrie Frankel has personally guaranteed me a role in *Wuthering Heights*, remember? As soon as it goes back into rehearsal I'm moving out of the Crown Towers and into my own place. I respect myself. I respect my body. I don't do drugs. And I haven't been with *anyone* since I left John." She came to a halt in the pathway, scrunching her mouth at me in that way of hers. "Listen, I don't know what your deal is but you don't have to worry about me, okay? I'm doing fine."

"Do they keep close tabs on you?"

She nodded. "On all of us. They'll start wondering where I am pretty soon. I'll tell them I decided to go shopping. It'll be okay."

"No, it won't. I wouldn't go back there if I were you."

"I *live* there. My stuff is there. Besides, I like what I'm doing. Why can't you just accept that?"

"Because I know more than you do."

Boso peered at me suspiciously. "What do you know?"

"I know that the law's going to land on those guys. They'll land on you, too, if you don't get out of there."

"You're not listening to me! I just told you, I'm *gittin'* out of there!" Farmer John was right. Her accent got thicker when she was pissed. "Morrie promised me I could understudy Isabella!"

I looked at her as she stood there in the park with her eyes blazing at me. Jonquil Beausoleil was no bimbo. She was smart and determined. A survivor. But she was also eighteen. She still had a lot to learn about the things that people do to each other.

"Morrie Frankel is a liar," I explained to her. "He lied to me. And he lied to you. He lies to pretty girls like you all of the time. Tells you anything you want to hear if he wants something from you. And he did want something—your help in staging this ruse of his. He's not going to cast you as an understudy in *Wuthering Heights*. That's never, ever going to happen."

"It will, too," she insisted angrily.

"No, it won't."

"He told me I'm genuinely gifted."

"Really? He told *me* that you're a 'showbiz tartlet' and a 'nothing.' He said, and I quote, 'You throw a stick on Jones Beach and you'll hit a hundred just like her.' Does that sound like a man who's going to give you a paying job in the biggest musical in Broadway history?"

Her big blue eyes were shiny now. Tears began to spill from them. "Why, that big, fat prick . . ."

"He's a big fat prick, all right."

"If he's been jerking me around I will make him so sorry."

"Really? How are you going to do that?"

"Don't worry, I'll find a way." She swiped the tears from her eyes and snuffled, shifting her clunky gym bag on her shoulder. "Nobody does shit like that to me and gets away with it! Nobody!" Then she went storming off.

"Wait, where are you going?"

"None of your danged business!"

"But I promised I'd take you back to Staten Island."

"You're not taking me anywhere. I'll call one of the boys to come get me."

"Wait a sec, *please*." I caught up with her and gave her my business card. "Call me any time. Day or night, okay?"

She peered at the card before she tore it in half and let the pieces flutter to the ground. Then she strode away, her shapely thighs churning, taut butt quivering. One, two, three different men swiveled their heads to watch her go by. Me, I wondered if I'd ever see her again. I did think about going after her. But what was I going to do, wrap her in duct tape and throw her in the trunk of my car? I couldn't stop her.

So instead I went to the Morley Hotel to see the great Morrie Frankel.

CHAPTER SIX

I COULD HEAR HIM hollering from out in the hotel hallway.

"You are under contract to *me*, you little limey fuck!" he roared as I tapped on his door. "Not Count Dracula, not Henderson, *me*. It's *my* show. The book belongs to me. The songs belong to me. *You* belong to me!"

Leah let me in, looking a bit flustered. "Morrie's on the phone," she whispered. "And he's not in a very good mood."

"That's okay. Neither am I."

"If you kids try to quit I'll sue you!" he screamed into his cell phone from the sofa, where he sat wearing another nylon jumpsuit, this one avocado green. Once again, he had a piece of Scotch tape stuck to his forehead. Once again, he had a huge portion of something sweet and gooey on the coffee table before him. Today it was Belgian waffles topped with blueberries and whipped cream. "If Count Dracula tries to go around me I'll sue him! If Henderson goes along I'll strangle *that* lying bastard with my bare hands! . . . Oh, yeah? Well, fuck you, too!" He hurled his cell phone against the living room wall. "I'm Morrie fucking Frankel!" he shouted at Leah, scarcely taking notice of me.

"Nobody steals *my* show and *my* stars! Do they honestly think I'm going to be pushed around by a couple of kids? The Matthew Puntigams and Hannah Lanes come and go. I don't. I'm eternal, you hear me?" He picked up the half-eaten plate of waffles and hurled that against the wall, too. "Eternal!"

Leah got busy cleaning it up, fussing and clucking.

"So it's *you,*" he snarled, glowering at me. "How dare you show your face here, you sniveling little rat."

"We need to have a talk, Mr. Frankel."

"*You* are a weasel," he blustered, rubbing his forehead irritably. When he remembered he was wearing a piece of Scotch tape there he yanked it off, tried to throw it away, couldn't, tried again, couldn't. So he stuck it on the coffee table. "*You* are a snake. Let me a throw a name at you—Cricket fucking O'Shea. I asked around and guess what? *You* were seen at Zoot Alors last night with that psychopathic little twat. Deny it. Go ahead. I dare you."

"Cricket and I went to school together." I sat down across the coffee table from him as Leah continued to tidy up. "I was hoping she might have a lead on Farnell."

Morrie looked at me suspiciously. "Did she?"

"I'm afraid not. She did tell me that Matthew can't sing a lick. And that Henderson Lebow was willing to lip-synch him but you refused."

"Damned right I did. This is Broadway. If we allow fakery to creep its way onstage then we are nothing. Matthew is no Bob Goulet, I'll grant you, but I believe the kid can pull it off. He's been getting top-notch voice coaching. And Henderson has been working with him for months. He's a bastard but he is one hell of a teacher."

"And what are you, Mr. Frankel? Aside from a total liar."

"What's that supposed to mean?"

"I found Jonquil Beausoleil. I've spoken with her."

"Already? That's terrific! Isn't that great, Leah? Benji found Farnell's little tootsie. Wow, kid, you're as good as they say. So where was she?"

"That's not important."

"Well, where's R.J.? Did you talk to him?"

"Are you done with this charade? Because it's getting to be kind of insulting. You sent Golden Legal Services on a wild goose chase, Mr. Frankel. She told me everything."

He furrowed his brow at me. "Everything as in . . . ?"

"As in there's no such person as R. J. Farnell."

Leah let out a gasp of shock as she stood there, soiled napkins in hand.

Morrie slumped on the sofa, rubbing a hand over his face. "Why would she say something like that?"

"Because she's in trouble. Not to mention really pissed at you."

"Pissed at me? Why?"

"You promised you were going to cast her as an understudy in *Wuthering Heights*, remember?"

He waved that off. "I was trying to encourage her. She's a kid."

"There's *no* R. J. Farnell?" Leah seemed genuinely flabbergasted.

"That's correct. You made him up, didn't you, Mr. Frankel? Concocted this whole elaborate story about a shadowy British hedge fund billionaire who promised to sink twelve million into your show. You had Boso rent the place in East Hampton on his behalf. And you pretended to be Farnell on the phone with the realtor, British accent and all, which I would really love to hear some time. A techie friend of Boso's set up the Web site for the Venusian Society, which is totally bogus. It's all been bogus. Why'd you do it, Mr. Frankel? And why on earth did you hire us to go looking for him? What were you hoping to accomplish?"

Morrie wouldn't answer me. Just sat there in surly silence.

Leah said it one more time: "There's *no* R. J. Farnell?"

"He's a phantom, Leah," he admitted grudgingly.

"But Morrie, I—I gave you . . ."

"A hundred thou, I know."

"My *last* hundred thou. Because you promised me Farnell was going to come through for you. You lied to me, Morrie."

"You'll get it back times ten, I swear," he vowed. "We always land on our feet, don't we? We're family. And we're in this together. Look, I needed that money, okay? Otherwise nobody would've believed I had a new angel. I had to pay some bills. And rent that beach house. And make a show of driving out there for the day, having lunch, acting like I was rolling in dough. I had to keep up the front. And now I need for you to stay positive, Leah. I need for you to believe in me. We'll have the hugest hit in Broadway history on our hands just as long as we both keep believing. Don't doubt me, Leah. Not after all these years. Please, I'm begging you."

Leah stood there breathing in and out for a long moment. "All right, Morrie," she said finally, sounding weary and defeated. "Whatever you say."

"That's my girl," he said brightly. "Now please leave us alone, will you?"

"Yes, Morrie."

I watched her go scuffing off to her office, her shoulders hunched. "I repeat, Mr. Frankel, what were you hoping to accomplish?"

"I needed to buy myself time, okay? Joe gave me two weeks to come up with some new backers—or else."

"Is Joe Minetta in on this with you? Does he know there's no R. J. Farnell?"

Reluctantly, Morrie nodded his head. "I said to him, Joe, my cupboard is bare. All I've got left is the old phantom angel ruse. I learned it from my mom, Benji. Haven't used it in thirty years, because it's such long odds. First you put out the word that you've found yourself a new, deep-pocketed money guy. Then this deep-pocketed money guy vanishes, leaving a trail of breadcrumbs behind. And then you get down on your knees and pray that somebody else steps forward with major cash while you're busy following the breadcrumbs. It's a major gamble. But I'm a major gambler. So is Joe, especially with my money and my show. All I needed from him was a girl. He grabbed me one of Little Joe's webcam bimbos. A budding actress, no less. She'd even shown up for our cattle call." He glared at me across the coffee table. "I can't believe you found her already. I was positive it would take you two weeks."

"You were wrong."

"But Joe told me those webcam girls are impossible to find. Little Joe keeps them stashed somewhere nobody knows about."

"Yeah, well, Little Joe may not be the sharpest knife in the drawer. There's also a distinct possibility that you were right yesterday—you *are* slipping. I'm curious, Mr. Frankel. Why did you choose Golden Legal Services? There are plenty of other detective agencies in the city."

"I wanted to be able to say I'd hired the best there is at finding missing young people. And the girl *swore* to me she'd play along. How did you get the truth out of her?"

"That's my job. It's what I do. Boso's in over her head, Mr. Frankel. She's gotten herself mixed up with organized crime. So have you."

"Joe's not 'organized crime,'" Morrie scoffed. "He's a businessman just like me. He's bailed me out plenty of times. And I've always paid him back. But I'm in real trouble with this show, no getting around it. So I put my chips on a phantom angel and now I'm scrambling like crazy to scare up new investors."

"How's that working out for you?"

Morrie puffed out his cheeks, Dizzy Gillespie style. "I've had plenty of new people step up, just like I told you yesterday. But . . . they're small timers. A few grand here, a few grand there. I need the big players, except they won't give me the time of day because that vampire Ira Gottfried's been whispering in the right ears that he's getting ready to swoop in and take over. Meanwhile, he's telling Matthew and Hannah that he won't produce the movie version of *Wuthering Heights* if Panorama doesn't own the play. It's grand theft, but they don't understand that. They're just kids."

"And where does Mr. Lebow fit in?"

"Henderson will do anything to direct *Wuthering Heights*, which will never, ever happen as long as I'm producing it. So he's thrown in with Count Dracula. No surprise there. Henderson is a man who has no concept of personal morality whatsoever. Plus he's desperate to get back at me." Morrie sat there in heavy silence for a moment. "Benji, I've never been this close to losing everything. I'm fighting for my life here. These people want to *destroy* me."

"I'm sorry to hear that, Mr. Frankel. I wish you luck. Really, I do." I got up off the sofa and started for the door. "We'll be sending you an itemized accounting of our expenses tomorrow."

His bulging eyes widened. "Wait, where are you going?"

"I'm quitting. Golden Legal Services no longer works for you."

"Nobody walks out on Morrie fucking Frankel!" he blustered at me. "Sit your little butt back down!"

I stayed on my feet. "Golden Legal Services is a respected, professional agency, Mr. Frankel. High-ranking people at One Police Plaza recommend our services."

"Is there a point to this?" he demanded.

"You hired us to find an actress who was pretending to be the girlfriend of a man who doesn't exist."

"I just told you, I was trying to buy myself a couple of weeks. What do you care? I paid you."

"You used us. You used Boso. You even used Leah, who's been your closest associate for, what, fifty years?"

"Fine, go ahead and slink out that door," he snarled at me. "But I want the balance of your advance back. There's no way you spent all five thou."

"Good luck with that."

"And if so much as one word of this ends up on *crickoshea.com* I swear I'll strangle you! Leah, get this Judas out of here!" he hollered. "Get him out, you hear me? Get! Him! Out!"

She came rushing from her office. "What's the problem, Morrie?"

"This little pisher is no longer in our employ. Get rid of him, will you? I've got some calls to make. And where's my goddamned phone?"

"You broke it, remember? Here, use mine." Leah handed him her cell before she ushered me out into the hotel's hallway. "Please believe me, Benji, I had no idea what Morrie was up to. If I had I would've tried to stop him." She lowered her eyes to the frayed carpet. "I guess that's why he didn't tell me."

"Leah, I can't turn this fucking phone on!" he roared from the living room.

"It *is* on!"

"Like hell it is!"

"Give me one second, Morrie!" She mustered a faint smile at me. "I'm sorry things didn't work out."

"Please explain one thing to me, Leah. How have you managed to put up with him for so many years? I barely lasted twenty-four hours."

"You're just catching him at a really bad time," she explained. "Morrie has a genuinely good heart. He's generous. He's brilliant. He's passionate. Besides, we have to make allowances for men like Morrie."

"We do? How come?"

"Leah, I am telling you this fucking phone is *not* on!"

"How come?" Leah glanced over her shoulder at the doorway, her face drawn tight with strain. "Because Morrie Frankel *is* Broadway."

I WAS PERCHED on a stool at a table in the front window of Gregory's, a gourmet coffee place that was across the street from the Morley. I sipped an iced Peruvian blend. I watched the hotel's front entrance. I waited.

More than an hour had passed since I'd left Morrie's suite and his employ. I'd phoned Mom to tell her that we were off the case, which she was totally fine with. Mom likes being played even less than I do. And now I sat there and watched the hotel and waited. I don't know if I was nursing a personal grudge or what. But I had a strong gut feeling that there was a whole lot more to this case, and that if I tailed the great Morrie Frankel he'd lead me to it.

Besides, I didn't have anywhere else to be.

I had to wait another hour before he came waddling out the door of the hotel wearing his avocado-colored jumpsuit, white sneakers with Velcro closures and a pair of outlandishly garish sunglasses that looked as if they'd once belonged to Sir Elton John. Morrie paused a second to say something to the doorman, who let out a big laugh. Then he started off in the direction of Sixth Avenue.

I followed him in the brutal midday heat, staying a safe two hundred yards back. Even though the sidewalks were crowded with people, Morrie was easy to spot in that jumpsuit. He turned left at the corner of Sixth Avenue and plodded his fat self down

Sixth past the International Center of Photography and the mammoth Bank of America Tower. He did not walk with ease. His toes pointed outward and he listed from side to side like a ship bobbing on a stormy sea. There was a Starbucks on the near corner of 42nd Street, but he wasn't going to Starbucks. He crossed 42nd Street and headed his way into Bryant Park.

Bryant Park, which backs up on the historic main branch of the New York Public Library on Fifth Avenue, used to be a crime-infested hole filled with rats of both the rodent and human variety. Office workers skulked in there to buy drugs in broad daylight. Absolutely no one went in there at night. Now it's so spruced up that it's one of midtown's most celebrated attractions.

In order to reach the park's emerald-green lawn Morrie had to make his way between the bustling, ornate 'Wichcraft Express kiosks that sell sandwiches, pastries, coffee and what not. Also past the cluster of Ping-Pong tables where animated young professionals were playing with lusty vigor, their neckties tucked smartly inside their shirts. Everywhere I go these days people are playing Ping-Pong. When did this happen? And why didn't I get the memo? Very few people were sprawled out on the lawn catching rays. Too damned hot out for that. But plenty of them were seated at the green Parisian-style park tables in the shade of the London plane trees that surround the lawn.

Morrie waddled his way to a table where a man sat waiting for him. He parked his fanny on a slatted folding chair, shifting himself this way and that, and the two of them began to talk. I moved behind a plane tree and used the zoom on my Nikon D80 to get a close-up view.

The man who Morrie was chatting with was slim and impeccably groomed. His silver hair was beautifully coiffed. His manicured fingernails gleamed. He had on an elegant white linen suit and an open-collar pale-green dress shirt. He wore the jacket thrown over his shoulders like a cape, a highly affected Continental look that very few American men can pull off.

Joe Minetta pulled it off.

Joe Minetta was a famously careful man. He never carried a phone or electronic device because they can be bugged. And he always conducted business outdoors in open public spaces. As I watched him I noticed that whenever he spoke to Morrie he raised a hand to his mouth so that no one could read his lips. I also noticed that he was not alone. A matched pair of bruisers with buzz cuts was seated at a nearby table. Bodyguards. I panned around the park to see if anyone else besides me was interested in the conversation between Morrie Frankel and Joe Minetta. I saw no one watching them. Or pretending not to watch them. I saw no one on the roof of the library. No one anywhere. If Sue Herrera had a crew on Joe they were very good.

The conversation between them seemed pleasant enough. Morrie did wave his arms in the air a bit, but that was just Morrie being Morrie. Joe seemed calm and collected. It was a brief conversation. Less than ten minutes. And when it was over they shook hands, smiled and parted amicably.

Joe sauntered off in the direction of the library with an unlit cigar between his fingers—there's no smoking in the park—and his jacket still draped over his shoulders. He seemed to be in no hurry to get anywhere. His bodyguards followed him like a pair of well-trained rottweilers.

Morrie took a bluestone path that led out of the park onto 42nd Street midway between Fifth and Sixth, directly across the street from the SUNY College of Optometry. I stayed with him as he turned left and started his way back toward Sixth amongst the tourists and street vendors who crowded the sidewalk. I was maybe a hundred yards behind him when a white Lincoln Navigator with tinted windows came our way from Sixth and pulled up next to him, stopping at the curb. He strolled right on by it, paying it no notice. The Navigator's passenger door opened and someone hopped out. Someone wearing a pair of wraparound shades, a baggy gray hoody with its hood up, baggy gray sweatpants and running shoes. Someone smallish and slim of build, though the sweats made it hard to tell just how slim. Someone who came up swiftly behind Morrie, raised an arm and shot him once, twice, three times in the back from less than three feet away with a nickel-plated 9mm semiautomatic handgun. A Smith & Wesson by the look of it. Not a quiet weapon. Everyone heard it. And at least two-dozen people were close enough to see it happen. Many of those people screamed as Morrie fell face-first to the pavement and stayed there while the shooter jumped back in the Navigator, leaving the shell casings behind on the sidewalk. I swiveled around and snapped a photo of the Navigator's license plate as its driver floored it toward Fifth Avenue, where it made a screeching right turn and disappeared around the corner heading downtown.

The entire hit took no more than ten seconds.

Someone had turned Morrie over. I knelt beside him as he lay there, gasping and gurgling, his eyes bulging blindly.

"Who was it, Morrie? Who did it?"

He grabbed me by my shirt and tried to speak, but couldn't. Then he shuddered violently and was gone.

The great Morrie Frankel was wrong. He wasn't eternal.

CHAPTER SEVEN

BY THE TIME LEGS GOT THERE the first responders from Midtown South had already cordoned off the crime scene. The techies were photographing and tagging any and all evidence. The M.E.'s man was attending to the late, great Morrie Frankel. These were people who moved fast, heat wave or no heat wave. So was Cricket, who showed up less than sixty seconds after the first responders did.

"Cricket, how on earth did you get here already?"

"I have my sources at Midtown South," she informed me as she snapped an iPhone picture of Morrie lying there dead on the sidewalk. "Talk to me, cutie. What happened?"

"Somebody shot him."

"Did you see it happen?"

"I saw it."

Her eyes gleamed at me eagerly. "And . . . ?"

"I have nothing to say, Cricket."

She swatted my arm. "Come on, Benji. I was your first sweetie. Doesn't that count for anything?"

"You mean aside from a lot of awkward memories? This

investigation isn't going to get cracked on your Web site. Just forget it, okay?"

"Why are you being such a butthead?"

"Maybe because I really don't like it when a client dies in my arms."

"Can I quote you on that?"

"Go away, Cricket."

She went away. Began talking to some of the tourists who'd witnessed the shooting. By now an army of TV news crews was arriving in vans, one after another after another.

And then I realized that Legs was standing next to me on the sidewalk. I wasn't surprised to see him there. Broadway's most famous producer had just been gunned down on 42nd Street in broad daylight in front of dozens of witnesses. The mayor would want to know that Commissioner Dante Feldman cared enough to send his very best.

Legs Diamond has six years and seven inches on me. Back when he joined the force out of Brooklyn College my dad took an interest in him. Changed his diapers and whispered in the right ears when Legs wanted to make detective. He knew that Legs was someone super smart. Someone who wasn't afraid to ruffle feathers. Someone special.

"What have you got for me, little bud?"

"One dead client named Morrie Frankel. I was tailing him."

"What was he doing?"

"Having a brief, polite conversation in the park with Joe Minetta."

Legs raised his eyebrows. "You don't say."

"I do say."

He thought this over, the secretaries and shop girls in their summer dresses casting lingering looks at him as they sidled their way around the police cordon. Legs is a guy who gets stared at by women. He has a lot of wavy black hair, soulful dark eyes and a goatee. He was wearing a black T-shirt that was molded to his wiry frame, tight jeans and motorcycle boots. Legs is kind of my idol in the looks department. Kind of my idol, period. The only thing I don't envy about him is his hyper-intensity. The man never relaxes.

"Did Frankel hire you to tail him?" he asked me, his right knee jiggling, jiggling.

"Not exactly. It was my own idea. In fact, he un-hired me a couple of hours ago, or tried to. I'd already quit."

"Okay, we'll get to that in a sec. What did you see?"

"A white Navigator with tinted windows pulled up. A shooter in full Unabomber regalia, on the small side, jumped out of the front passenger seat, shot him three times in the back from close range, jumped back in and the Navigator took off down Fifth. I gave your people the license number." My eyes scanned the buildings directly across the street. "The College of Optometry will have security cams in the lobby. So will the Banco do Brasil. And that's just for starters, am I right?"

He peered at me. "Where are you going with this?"

"You know exactly where I'm going. The CCTV cameras. The ones that no one talks about."

"True that," he conceded. "There are closed-circuit surveillance cameras covering every highly populated section of midtown. It's a Homeland Security thing. And this is freaking Bryant Park. So, yeah, we'll have footage up the wazoo. It'll take a lot of eyeballs a lot of hours but we'll be able to track where that Navigator was before the shooting and where it went afterward, no doubt. You said Frankel un-hired you?"

"I said I quit."

"Why did he hire you in the first place?"

"He was drowning in debt. Wanted us to find a Mr. R. J. Farnell, a British hedge fund player who was supposed to save *Wuthering Heights* for him. It turned out that Farnell was a phantom angel, as in Morrie made him up. He made up a girlfriend for us to look for, too. Was hoping to buy himself a couple of weeks to raise the money he needed. He brought us on board to provide him with cover. It was a crap case. I bailed."

"So why were you following him?"

"I don't like to be used."

He flashed a grin at me. "You're just like your father, know that?"

"The shooter's weapon looked like a nickel-plated Smith & Wesson 9 mil to me. That's not a particularly lightweight weapon, is it?"

"Weighs maybe a pound and a half. Why are you asking?"

"No reason in particular."

He studied me closely. "Let's widen out here. Could Joe Minetta have been the intended target?"

"That's a no. Joe Minetta took off in the other direction when they parted company. He was way over by the library when it went down."

"Any chance that it was Minetta who arranged the hit?"

"That's a yes. Except no."

"Why not?"

"Joe Minetta's a big-time Broadway loan shark. A loan shark doesn't kill a producer who owes him money. He takes his show away from him. Minetta would have to be a hotheaded idiot to gun down Morrie, especially on a crowded midtown sidewalk less than five minutes after they parted company. And Minetta is no hotheaded idiot."

Legs thumbed his goatee thoughtfully. "And yet Frankel was rubbed out pro style by a shooter and driver who knew exactly where to find him. How on earth would they know that unless they were tipped off?"

"I have no idea, Legs. But you're right. They were waiting for him."

"Which tells me that either Minetta ordered the hit or that you weren't the only one who was following Frankel. Did you spot anybody else?"

"That's a no."

"Did you see Minetta signal anybody?"

"That's also a no. You really think he ordered the hit?"

"Well, yeah. Unless you've got another way of selling it to me. In which case please do. Who else would want to take out a Broadway legend like Morrie Frankel?"

"You mean besides virtually everyone who knew him?"

Legs frowned at me. "So it's like that, is it?"

"Yeah, it's like that."

"OMG, it's Legs Diamond!" Cricket burbled excitedly as she charged her way over toward us. "Now we are talking *serious* big time! What can you tell us, Legs?"

He looked at her blankly. "Who is *us*?"

"My readers, Legs. I get hundreds of thousands of hits a day."

"And you are . . . ?"

"Meet Cricket O'Shea," I said to him.

"You're *the* Cricket?" Legs studied her with keen interest now. "I remember Benji talking about you back when you two were an item."

Her face lit up. "Really? What did he say about me?"

"Sorry, that's in the guy vault. Tell me, *the* Cricket, how'd you get inside of our crime scene perimeter?"

"I started out inside of your crime scene perimeter, that's how. So who do you think shot Morrie, Legs? What's your working theory?"

"I don't have one. Just got here. But, hey, feel free to share yours."

"Who, me? Glad to. I say there's a sixty-five-million-dollar Broadway musical that was ready to lift off the ground and Morrie was holding it back. I say that one of its principals made sure he couldn't do that anymore. That's just this reporter's opinion, Legs, but can I say that *you* said it? I'll call you an unnamed source with intimate knowledge of the investigation. How would that be?"

"Would it do any good if I said no freaking way?"

"None." She batted her eyelashes at him. "One more question—would you please be the father of my first child?"

"Go away, Cricket," I said.

She went away, thumbing out a tweet as she darted off.

Legs grinned at me. "So that's *the* Cricket. She's kind of cute, in a deranged sort of way."

"Are you enjoying yourself?"

"Hugely. In fact, I'd say my day has been made." He narrowed his eyes at me, back to business. "You said Frankel made up a girlfriend for you to look for. Did you find her?"

I nodded. "Jonquil Beausoleil, an aspiring actress who was a high-school cheerleader in Ruston, Louisiana until she ran away from home four months ago."

"Hence your involvement."

"Hence my involvement. Boso—she calls herself Boso—is currently appearing daily and nightly as a webcam girl for various Internet porn sites that the Minettas operate out of a high-rise apartment building in Staten Island. That's how I ran into your friend Sue Herrera of OCCB this morning. They have the building under surveillance."

"How did this girl get mixed up with Frankel?"

"Morrie needed a girl. Joe Minetta got him one. Morrie promised Boso an understudy role in *Wuthering Heights* if she'd pretend to be R. J. Farnell's girlfriend-slash-executive assistant. He told her he was playing a prank on a friend. She went along with it. Rented a shmancy beach house in East Hampton for him. But it was all one big lie—including the business about casting her in *Wuthering Heights*. He never had any intention of hiring that girl."

"Does she know that?"

"She knows it. I told her. I felt I owed it to her, one struggling actor to another. Besides, she's not a bad sort. Had herself a nice, rich boyfriend until a few weeks ago. The guy's crazy about her. But you know how that goes."

"Meaning she's damaged goods?"

"To the bone."

"Her scumbag father?"

"Her scumbag stepfather."

"How did she take it when you set her straight about Frankel?"

"Not well."

"Would you say she has a temper?"

"She has a temper."

"And when did you set her straight?"

"About three hours ago. We were in Central Park."

"Sounds to me like Boso could be a player."

"For a gangland style rubout? Get real."

"All it takes is a hoody, a Navigator and a dream."

"And a partner. It was a two-person job, remember?"

"You just told me she had a boyfriend who's crazy about her, remember?"

"That's right, I did," I had to admit.

"Any idea where she is right now?"

"None."

Legs mulled this over. "Who else had a beef with Frankel?"

"Matthew Puntigam and Hannah Lane. Morrie was screaming at Matthew on the phone when I showed up at his hotel to quit. Promised he'd sue if they tried to get out of their contract with him."

"Why would they want to do that?"

"Because Ira Gottfried, their Panorama uber-boss, has been messing with their heads. Or so Morrie claimed."

"Messing with their heads as in . . . ?"

"Telling them Panorama will never make a film version of *Wuthering Heights* unless it owns the stage rights. Which it doesn't. Morrie wouldn't let Gottfried within ten feet of his show.

He was the last of the independents. Gottfried's not someone who takes no for an answer. He's recruited Henderson Lebow, who was the show's original director until Morrie punched him out and fired him. The four of them—Ira Gottfried, Henderson Lebow, Matthew Puntigam and Hannah Lane—made a very public show of having dinner together last night at Zoot Alors. It made Morrie froth at the mouth. Oh, and it may interest you to know that Morrie and Henderson were lovers until Morrie caught Henderson two-timing him with a certain younger man. Now you'll want to ask me who this younger man is."

"Okay, who is he?"

"Matthew Puntigam."

Legs blinked at me. "Aren't he and Hannah Lane a couple?"

"They are."

"So Matthew Puntigam is . . . ?"

"British," I said, nodding.

"I was going to say bisexual. What's him being British have to do with anything?"

"All British actors are switch-hitters, according to Cricket." I watched her as she flitted around the crime scene asking questions and snapping pictures. She was so full of moxie that it didn't occur to anyone that she belonged outside of the cordon with all of the other media people. "And she's one of the theater world's five most influential people, according to the Styles section of *The New York Times*. So it must be true."

Legs responded to this with a sour grunt, his right knee jiggling, jiggling as we stood there in the suffocating heat. "So what we have here is the brazen midtown shooting of a Broadway legend in broad daylight during the height of the tourist season *and* pretty much everyone who's involved is famous. The mayor is going to be calling Commissioner Feldman ten times a day. Which means Feldman will be calling me *twenty* times a day."

"I know. Sorry, Legs."

He patted me on the shoulder. "No prob, little bud. This is how I roll. I think I'm up to speed now, although I'm still a tiny bit confused about one thing. This British hedge fund player, R. J. Farnell . . ."

"What about him?"

"Is he real or not?"

"There is no such person as R. J. Farnell."

"Got it. I'm all good now." His cell phone rang. Legs glanced at its screen and took the call. Listened. Listened some more. Then said, "Okay, we'll be there." Then he rang off and said, "It's getting stankier. We've both been summoned to 26 Federal Plaza." That happened to be the address of the New York City field office of the FBI. "Let's ride."

"Whatever you say. We just have to make one quick stop on the way."

LEAH HAD ALREADY HEARD the news. The television in the suite's living room was tuned to CNN's live coverage of the shooting.

"Why would anyone want to hurt *Morrie*?" she asked me forlornly as she sat there on the sofa, clutching a wadded tissue in her hand. Her face was flushed, her eyes red. The woman was devastated. "How will *Wuthering Heights* go on without him? How will *I* go on? God, what will I do?"

I reached for the remote and muted the sound. "You'll keep

on going," I said to her consolingly. "That's what we do, Leah. We have to. Didn't you mention that you have a son who lives in Williamsburg?"

She swallowed, nodding her head. "Charlie."

"Would you like us to call him for you?"

"Thank you. I'll call him myself in a—a little while." Leah dabbed at her nose with the tissue, gazing across the coffee table at me. "You're being very sweet, considering the way Morrie talked to you. It was just noise, you know. He didn't mean half of what came out of his mouth. That was just Morrie's way. We worked together, side by side, our whole lives. He was my best friend. We were a team. We were . . ." She let out a pained sob. "I'm sorry, I'm babbling like a crazy woman, aren't I? I—I just can't believe he's gone. Why would *anyone* want to do this to him?"

"That's what Lieutenant Diamond's going to find out."

"May I ask you a couple of questions?" Legs said to her. "Or I can come back later if you don't feel up to it right now."

"No, no, I'm fine." Leah sat up straighter in her trim linen dress, willing herself back to a state of crisp, professional composure. "Ask me anything, Lieutenant. I want to help."

"Were you in on this R. J. Farnell scam with Mr. Frankel?"

"No, I was not. Morrie didn't tell me every single thing he was doing. How could he? That man came up with new ideas in his sleep. And he . . . did keep secrets from me," she admitted, lowering her eyes.

"He lied to you, you mean," I said. "He promised you Farnell would come through for him. That's how he convinced you to give him your last hundred thou, isn't it?"

"Well, yes," Leah allowed.

"That had to be hard," Legs said.

"Not at all," she responded sharply. "I was accustomed to Morrie's ways. You'd be amazed at what can seem normal after a while, Lieutenant. Besides, Morrie needed that money desperately. He wasn't worth a cent. All he had were debts. There'll be creditors lined up around the block tomorrow morning."

"How much did he owe Joe Minetta?" Legs asked her.

"Millions. Don't ask me how many. I don't know."

"Was there anything on paper? Did Mr. Frankel ever sign a promissory note?"

"Never. It was strictly cash and a handshake with Joe. Which was fine by Morrie. He liked doing business that way, too. I used to keep tens of thousands in cash downstairs in the hotel's safe. Not anymore. All that's left is a few hundred dollars in my office strongbox. And would you believe he owed the Morley three months back rent on this suite?" She looked around at the worn furniture and food-stained walls. "They could have kicked him out if they'd wanted to, but they took pity on him. *Pity.* That's how far he'd fallen. Such a great, great producer. They should name a theater after him. No one gave more to Broadway than Morrie Frankel did. I—I wonder if they'll even dim the lights on the marquees for him tonight."

"That's the traditional Broadway tribute when someone of his stature passes away," I said. "I'm sure they will."

She looked at me surprised. "Really? I'm not. The other producers all hated him, you know. Morrie didn't just burn bridges. He dynamited them. I'll . . . try to keep the office open for the time being. I'll be getting phone calls from the press. And the lawyers and agents will be calling. *Wuthering Heights* was his last great discovery. And the show must go on, right?" Leah let out a mournful sigh, her resolve crumbling. "My God, will you listen to me? There is no *Wuthering Heights*. Or at least not with this company's participation. Not now. Not ever."

"Why not, Leah?"

"Because Matthew and Hannah were under contract to Morrie Frankel Productions. And Morrie Frankel Productions owned the rights to the book, the music, lyrics. Morrie *was* Morrie Frankel Productions. He was a one-man band. There was no organization, no chain of succession. Just Morrie."

"And I'm guessing," Legs said slowly, "that all of those very talented people have very smart lawyers who made absolutely sure they inserted an out-clause in case anything unfortunate should happen to that one-man band."

"Naturally," Leah said. "With Morrie gone those contracts will be voided. Matthew and Hannah will be free to sign with anyone else they choose. The whole creative team will be. Do you understand what I'm saying to you? These awful people who shot Morrie did more than just kill him. They did something ten times worse. They stole his show out from under him."

"DO YOU THINK that's why he was killed?"

"Don't you?" I said, holding on for dear life as we rocketed down Fifth Avenue in Legs' dented, sprung Crown Vic. Pedal to the metal is the only way he knows how to drive—slowpokes, delivery vans and potholes be damned.

"It plays in terms of motive, that's for damned sure. Except I've got a couple of problems, such as—"

"Why bother," I said, nodding. "Morrie was already circling the drain. Why not just wait for him to lose *Wuthering Heights* on his own?"

"Well, yeah."

"What's your other problem?"

"The shooting. It has the outward appearance of being a professional hit, except it's what I call a disorganized homicide."

"Disorganized as in . . . ?"

"Busy street, lots of witnesses. It was planned, no question. But pros like to work in the quiet and the dark. And they don't like witnesses." Legs brooded in silence for a moment before he said, "What'll happen to that lady?"

"Leah's a top theatrical assistant. My guess? Somebody will find a place for her."

"And what about *Wuthering Heights*?"

"That I don't have to guess about. Ira Gottfried will take it over and Panorama will make a fortune. Just think how much free publicity this show's about to get. Morrie's murder is a tabloid dream. It's huge, Legs."

"Huge," Legs agreed as he sped past Madison Square Park toward the Flatiron Building. At 23rd Street he veered left onto Broadway. His cell phone rang. He took the call. Listened. Listened some more. Then said, "Okay, good. Thanks." Rang off and said, "They used a license plate reader to track the Navigator. It left Manhattan through the Queens-Midtown Tunnel less than a half hour after the shooting. Came in through the very same tunnel from Queens at seven minutes after ten this morning."

"Who owns it?"

"A housewife in Bayside. She reported it stolen out of a Waldbaum's parking lot in Flushing shortly before nine o'clock." Legs glanced across the seat at me. "How's your mom doing?"

"She's good. Stop by and say hi. She misses you."

"I miss her, too. Abby's one of the great ones. And what's up with Rita?"

"She's seeing a dentist named Myron."

"So you two aren't together anymore?"

"We were never 'together.' We were just a couple of friends helping each other through a rough patch."

He flashed a grin at me. "Rita's six feet tall. She's totally hot. She used to be a lap dancer. And you're making it sound like it was no big deal, you player. Hell, I can remember when you were afraid to ask little Cricket out on a date. Although now that I've met her I can see why."

"Legs, I was a whole lot younger then."

"Dude, it was three years ago."

"Don't exaggerate. It was five. Okay, four. And how about you?" Legs is a lone wolf. His longest relationship lasted three weeks. "What's up between you and Sue Herrera of OCCB?"

"What makes you think anything is?"

"You cock-blocked me when I mentioned her name to you on the phone."

"That wasn't a cock-block. That was a friendly warning. She's toting excess baggage—an eight-year-old daughter *and* a restraining order against her ex, Richie, who's on the job and has anger management issues, as in he likes to beat the crap out of Sue whenever he gets loaded. It's a package deal. And it's not for me. *She's* not for me. So let's just drop the subject," he growled. "Why are we even talking about this?"

"Because you brought it up."

"Watch yourself, cowboy. I can still pound the snot out of you."

"Don't be so sure. I've got some wicked new moves."

Our destination, 26 Federal Plaza—officially known as the Jacob K. Javits Federal Office Building—is a huge fortress of granite and glass that's located across Foley Square from the New York County Courthouse. There are concrete bollards placed strategically outside of the building to keep car bombers from getting any ideas. And there are checkpoints galore. We had to pass through three of them in order to reach the FBI's offices up on the 23rd floor.

The meeting we'd been summoned to didn't take place in somebody's private office. Or in one of those formal conference rooms where a bunch of Very Serious People sit around a long table while another Very Serious Person delivers a PowerPoint presentation. No, we met in a small, windowless room that would have served nicely as a break room if it had a refrigerator and a microwave. Which it didn't.

Three people were crammed in there waiting for us. One was our good friend Sue Herrera, who looked exceedingly tense. One was an FBI Special Agent named Jack Dytman, who was maybe thirty-five, skinny and bucktoothed, with flaky hair of no particular color and a heat rash on his neck that looked itchy and angry and just plain awful. I mean it, the man's neck looked like raw ground round. Dytman was also the possessor of a truly damp handshake. My dad taught me to never, ever trust a man who has a truly damp handshake. The third person was Gino Cimoli, a U.S. Attorney for the Eastern District of New York

City, which means Brooklyn, Queens and Staten Island. Cimoli was in charge. He let us know this by staying on his feet, one foot planted firmly on an empty chair, while the rest of us were seated. He had a cocky, blustery air about him. Which was to be expected. Federal prosecutors don't tend to be shrinking violets. Purple people eaters is more like it. Think Chris Christie. Think Rudy Giuliani. Don't think matinee idol. Cimoli was tubby, jowly and a bona fide chrome dome. He was also in need of a serious style makeover by Joe Minetta. The man's dark gray Zegna knockoff didn't help him one bit. The pants were way too roomy in the seat. Plus he wore an unstylish sneer on his face that I'm guessing had been there since the first time he went away to sleepover camp and got tagged with the nickname of Lumpy. Cimoli was trying real hard to impress Sue Herrera. I know this because he was sucking in his stomach and puffing out his chest. He had no chance. Not with Legs in the room. None.

"There are some questions we need to ask you, Mr. Golden," he began gruffly. "And we expect honest answers."

"Do I need to call my honest lawyer?"

"That wouldn't be a good idea."

"Why not?"

"Because that would mean that we were actually having this conversation. Do we understand each other?"

"Not really, but I'm kind of slow."

"It means that what happens in Vegas stays in Vegas," Special Agent Dytman said, craning his itchy neck.

I looked at Legs. "Did you bring your decoder ring?"

"Afraid not."

"We just need to know what you bad boys are into," Sue

explained, her dark eyes gleaming at Legs. "We're all on the same side. We can play nice, can't we?"

Legs smiled at her. "I always play nice, Suzy Q."

She smiled back at him. "That's true, you do."

Cimoli glared at them. Dytman craned his itchy neck some more, fingering it gingerly. Me, I was starting to miss sitting in my parked car in the hot sun on Staten Island. I'd been alone with my thoughts. I could listen to Ethel Merman. Life was good then.

"Jonquil Beausoleil," Cimoli barked at me. "Where is she?"

"How would I know?"

"You slipped your tail, Benji," Sue said scoldingly.

"You're not going to slap me around again, are you?"

Legs' eyes widened. "She slapped you?"

"Where'd you take her?" Sue asked me.

"For a walk in Central Park. And I didn't tip your play, if that's what you're freaking out about."

"What *did* you do?" Dytman asked me.

"Gave her the usual speech I give to eighteen-year-old runaways who find themselves in her position—get out of the business now or you'll end up becoming a prostitute."

"*End up* becoming a prostitute?" Cimoli let out a harsh laugh. "What do you think she is now?"

"A high school cheerleader from Ruston, Louisiana," I said to him.

"Then what happened?" Sue asked me.

"We parted company. She told me she'd have one of the Crown Towers boys come pick her up. That was the last I saw of her."

"When was this?"

"Why are you so interested in her?"

"Because it so happens that everyone else is home," Sue explained. "Every single one of the boys and girls is tucked in at the Crown Towers as we speak. Everyone except for Jonquil Beausoleil."

"Where is she?" Cimoli demanded.

"I just told you. I left her in the park."

"And when was this?" Sue asked me again.

"Early this afternoon." It was now after five o'clock.

"Are you purposely being vague?" Dytman asked me.

"Who's being vague?" Legs demanded. "Isn't it about time you told us why we're here?"

Sue Herrera looked at Jack Dytman who looked at Gino Cimoli. He gave Dytman a brief nod.

Dytman cleared his throat and said, "For the past several months we've been conducting a joint FBI-NYPD investigation into illegal activities that are headquartered in the Crown Towers apartment building. Thousands of man-hours have been invested in this investigation, which has been dubbed Operation Yum-Yum for reasons that will soon become clear to you. We're now one hundred percent certain that we have the Minetta crime family nailed on a laundry list of RICO violations. We have all of our ducks in a row. And we have the green light. We're ready to move in and shut that whole criminal enterprise down. The manpower is literally on standby at this very minute."

Legs tugged at his goatee. "You're planning to raid the building?"

"In exactly . . . sixty-seven minutes," Dytman confirmed, glancing at his watch. "Unless you gentlemen give us a good reason not to."

Sue gazed at me inquiringly. "Benji, why do we keep running into each other? This morning you were at the Crown Towers looking for Jonquil Beausoleil. And this afternoon you were less than fifty feet from Morrie Frankel when he was gunned down after he met with Joe Minetta in Bryant Park."

"You were watching Joe Minetta? I didn't spot your people. Who . . . ?"

"Two young mothers with stroller cams," she replied. "Why were *you* there? We need to know why you were tailing Morrie Frankel. And why you were looking for Jonquil Beausoleil. And what the connection is, or I should say was, between her, Morrie Frankel and Joe Minetta. Legs, we know you've got a murder to investigate. What we don't know is whether our two cases have anything to do with each other."

"We've *got* to know if your murder investigation is going to compromise our operation," Cimoli huffed at him. "And I mean right fucking now."

"How would I know?" Legs huffed right back. "I haven't got the slightest idea what's been going on at the Crown Towers. Everything so far has been about you and what you need. Let's talk about me for a change. My job is to catch two people who just murdered Broadway's most famous producer in front of a gazillion horrified tourists, quite a few of them children who will never forget what they saw today. My job is *not* to sit in a glorified broom closet while some fat clown cake from DOJ tries to swing his inch-long dick at me. I've got things to do. So tell me, tell *us*, what the fuck is going on or we are out the door. Got it?"

Cimoli flushed a deep shade of red. I forgot to mention that you don't ever want to play the bully card with Legs. That's even more heinous than calling him Larry.

"Not one word we say here leaves this room," Sue cautioned me. "Do I have your word?"

"You do."

"How do we know he can be trusted?" Cimoli demanded.

"You don't have to know," Legs replied. "*I* know."

"Sure, that's fine," Dytman said placatingly. "Totally fine. Here's the deal, okay? We've been wiretapping the Crown Towers twenty-four/seven for some time now. The building's owned by the Minettas through a legitimate subsidiary known as—"

"Top Hat Property Management," I said. "I already know that."

"What you may not know," Dytman said, his nostrils flaring at me slightly, "is that Joe Minetta, Jr., better known as Little Joe, has put together an incredibly sophisticated and lucrative operation with his cousin Petey. These boys are college graduates with cutting-edge computer skills and loads of ingenuity. Just for starters, they're running an Internet porn empire out of the Crown Towers—or Little Joe's Yum-Yum Tree as we call it. Sixteen webcam girls are living there at all times. The boys have units there, too. The whole setup is like a frat boy's wet dream. And the porn sites are nice, solid earners. But they're strictly window dressing. The big money comes from something a whole lot nastier. Day in and day out they manage to convince hundreds of lonely, horny rubes out there to pony up thirty-nine bucks a month for extra-special membership in—"

"Their extra-special Gold Club or Premiere Club or whatever the hell they're calling it," I said, nodding my head.

Dytman flared his nostrils at me again. "Supposedly, this buys them exclusive access to all sorts of earthly delights. But do you know what it really means?"

"Let me take a wild guess," Legs said. "Do these lonely, horny rubes happen to pay by credit card?"

"Bingo," Sue said. "Two entire floors of the Crown Towers are devoted to a high-tech identity theft operation. We're talking state-of-the-art computers, scanners, encoders, embossing machines, the works. The instant they have access to a guy's credit card info they steal his ID and clean the sucker out. They move so fast and hard that they've maxed out his line of credit and moved on before the slob even knows what's hit him."

"They buy fancy merchandise," Dytman went on. "Rolex watches, Hermès handbags, Armani leather jackets. They've got a climate-controlled storage warehouse with seventeen thousand bottles of wine in it. They've got antique furniture. They've got paintings. I'm talking about mountains and mountains of loot that's stashed in Top Hat buildings all over Staten Island."

"And it's the girls who do a lot of the buying," Sue said. "The boys send them on shopping sprees to fancy stores with their wallets stuffed full of credit cards and driver's licenses. The girls love it. Makes them feel rich and sophisticated."

"It also makes them accessories to credit card fraud," Cimoli spoke up. "On top of whatever else they're already doing that's illegal, by which I mean high-end prostitution. A lot of those girls are on drugs, too."

"We don't know each other very well," I said to him. "So I'll try to put this to you tactfully. Please don't lump all of 'those girls' together, okay? Because they're not all the same, dickwad."

"It looks like a boy but it's a man," marveled Sue, who was amused.

Cimoli was not. "How would *you* know anything about it?"

"I have a family history."

"Meaning what?"

"Meaning let's move on," Legs growled impatiently.

"These boys are clever," Dytman continued. "They use the stolen credit cards and fake IDs to rent luxury cars, then they steal the cars and ship them out of state. They buy up tickets by the thousands and scalp them. You want front row seats to see Bruce Springsteen at Madison Square Garden? They've got them. We are talking about a highly organized, multimillion-dollar criminal enterprise. That, in a nutshell, is Operation Yum-Yum. Got it, Lieutenant?"

"Got it," Legs said. "And big ups for the catchy name."

Dytman ignored that remark, steering his attention back to me. "The ball's in your court now. Do you know where Jonquil Beausoleil is?"

"No."

"Would you tell us if you did?"

"I don't know. I don't like you people very much."

"Benji, what's her connection to Morrie Frankel?" Sue asked.

"He hired me to find her."

"Why?"

"That's a long story."

"We like long stories," she assured me.

"Love them," Dytman agreed, craning his itchy neck.

Cimoli just stood there with his foot on his chair, glowering at me. Possibly it had to do with my use of the word "dickwad."

"*Wuthering Heights* has been in serious financial trouble for months," I told them. "Morrie Frankel informed me that a British hedge fund billionaire named R. J. Farnell had promised to bail him out to the tune of twelve mil, but that Farnell had disappeared. The best lead he had on Farnell was the guy's girlfriend, an aspiring young actress named Jonquil Beausoleil. My associates and I were able to track her to the Crown Towers, where I approached her this morning and she informed me that there was, in fact, no such person as R. J. Farnell. He was a phantom angel, which is an old-time scam that Broadway showmen resort to when they're on the ropes. They invent a shadowy, deep-pocketed moneyman and use him as bait to draw in other investors. Morrie was hoping the ruse would buy him a couple of weeks to raise more money. All it bought him was twenty-four hours. That's how long it took us to find her."

"He shouldn't have hired the best," Legs said to me.

"He shouldn't have done a lot of things," I said. "Like tell Jonquil Beausoleil he'd cast her as an understudy in *Wuthering Heights* if she'd pretend to be Farnell's girlfriend. Which she was more than happy to do. She thought Morrie had just handed her the biggest break of her career."

"How did he come to choose her?" Sue asked me.

"He didn't. Joe Minetta put the two of them together."

"Why would Minetta do that?" Cimoli asked.

"Joe Minetta is the biggest loan shark on Broadway. You know that, right?"

They didn't respond. Just stared at me.

"Well, Morrie was in deep to him. Morrie's assistant, Leah Shimmel, told me that some knuckle draggers even came looking for Morrie at his hotel a couple of weeks ago. This phantom angel scam wasn't just Morrie's last, best hope of bringing *Wuthering Heights* to the stage. It was his way of trying to square things with Minetta."

Sue Herrera thought this over. "So you figure they were talking money in Bryant Park?"

"You tell us," Legs said. "You're the ones who had Minetta under surveillance."

"We're reviewing our stroller cams," she said. "But we generally don't learn a whole lot when it comes to that man. He's incredibly careful."

"He had two bodyguards parked at a nearby table," I said. "Did one of them use his cell phone after he and Morrie separated? Or signal anyone?"

Sue shook her head. "Not that we observed. But if Minetta arranged the hit then it's possible that it was already set up. No signal required. I can buy that."

"I can't," I said. "Every single day that Morrie was alive Minetta was gobbling up a bigger piece of *Wuthering Heights*. Now that Morrie's dead he gets nothing. Somebody else will take over the show. Somebody like Ira Gottfried of Panorama Studios, who couldn't care less about what Morrie owed Minetta—especially because there's nothing on paper. They did everything by handshake. Nope, I don't buy it. Minetta wanted Morrie alive."

"So who wanted him dead?" Dytman wondered.

"Awesome question," Legs snapped. "I'd like to know that myself. Are you people going to let me start my investigation?"

"Hey, our clock's ticking," Dytman reminded him, glancing at his watch. "We're down to forty-two minutes."

"And we've got to make sure we're all on the same page," Sue said. "Benji, why were you tailing Morrie Frankel in Bryant Park?"

"Because he hosed me."

"And are you sticking to this story that you don't know where Jonquil Beausoleil is?" Cimoli demanded.

"It's not a story. I don't know where she is."

"We need her in the house," he said, stabbing at the table with his blunt index finger. "If she's not home when we raid the Crown Towers then she's a loose end. And loose ends always come back to bite you in the ass."

"Let's say I can find her . . ."

"Let's," Sue said eagerly.

"What'll you offer her in exchange for her cooperation?"

"Are you suggesting immunity from prosecution?" Cimoli shook his head at me. "No way. We've got her dead to rights for credit card fraud. That's a federal crime. She'll have to plead out just like the other girls." He paused, running a hand over his chrome dome. "Unless she's got gold for us. And by that I mean game-changing information. If she has something like that we'd listen. Does she?"

"I honestly have no idea."

"This girl needs to be found," he reiterated, his voice rising with urgency.

"Agreed," Legs said. "Except I'm bringing her in, not you."

"Why?" Cimoli demanded.

"Because she's a person of interest in my homicide investigation."

"You're out of your league here, Lieutenant," Cimoli told him. "Need I point out that this is *federal*?"

"Need I point out that I don't give a shit? And neither will Commissioner Feldman." Legs reached for his cell. "Let's include him in your little pissing contest."

Cimoli's gaze hardened. "So you've got major juice at One PP. I know that. You don't have to show off."

"I'm not the one who's showing off," Legs said as the cell rang in his hand. He peered at the screen and took the call. Listened. Listened some more. Then said, "Okay, right." Rang off and got up out of his chair. "We just found the Navigator. They ditched it in Queens behind a beauty salon on Woodhaven Boulevard. I'd love to stay here and chat with you folks but I've got an actual job to do. You do yours, I'll do mine and as far as I'm concerned we have nothing more to talk about. Come on, Benji. Let's bounce."

"We're not done here, Lieutenant!" Cimoli roared at him.

Legs came to a halt, his right knee jiggling, jiggling.

"Here's how I'm reading the situation," Cimoli put forward. "This Beausoleil girl qualifies as a definite loose end. But she does not, in and of herself, constitute a concrete reason for us to hit the pause button on our raid. Let's say she turns out to be your Bryant Park shooter. So what? A Broadway producer lied to a young actress. The young actress got *really* pissed off at him. That's got nothing to do with us. Am I right, Lieutenant?"

Legs stood there thinking it over. Gino Cimoli waited anxiously for his reply. So did Jack Dytman and Sue Herrera. All three of them were gazing at him with expectant looks on their faces. It never fails to amaze me how *nobody* wants be the one who makes the final call. Fear of fucking up. Their lives are ruled by fear of fucking up.

"You want to know what I think?" Legs responded. "If I were you, what I'd be most concerned about right now is my murder investigation shining an unwanted light on your operation. Possibly even provoking the Minettas into cutting and running. My advice? Move in fast."

Dytman studied him carefully. "Proceed as planned, you mean?"

"Absolutely. Don't even think about it. Just do it." Legs let out an antsy sigh. "You need us for anything else?"

"You'll know it when we do," Cimoli answered with a sneer.

And with that Legs and I took off.

"I see a genuine bromance brewing between you and Cimoli," I said as we strode to the elevator. "Maybe even the three of you taking a trip to Barbados together—just you, Cimoli and Cimoli's ego."

"He's standard government issue," Legs said dismissively. "Big head, glass jaw. So, listen, I'll be humping the surveillance cams and forensics tonight. And I've got detectives paying courtesy calls on Matthew Puntigam and Hannah Lane, on Henderson Lebow and on Ira Gottfried. The NYPD's reaching out with kid gloves to answer any questions they might have about their near and dear friend Morrie Frankel." He punched the button for the elevator—once, twice, three times. "This way they'll be feeling kindly toward the department when I have a go at them myself tomorrow morning. I'll pick you up at nine. I want you by my side. You down with that?"

"Totally. Does this mean we're working the case together?"

"No, it means you actually comprehend who's screwing who and I don't."

"Sure sounds to me like we're working the case together."

"We're not working the case together."

"Whatever you say." The elevator arrived. We got in. I watched him punch the CLOSE DOOR button once, twice, three times before the door finally closed and we started riding down. "Anything I can do to help before then?"

"Yeah. It would be fairly huge if you could find Jonquil Beausoleil."

"Not a problem."

He raised his eyebrows at me. "You really think you can find her?"

"I found her once. I'll find her again."

Actually, it turned out to be a whole lot easier than I thought. I didn't have to find Boso at all. She found me.

CHAPTER EIGHT

SHE WAS SITTING ON Mom's office sofa in her cropped tank top and spandex shorts drinking a bottle of mineral water. Gus was sprawled next to her offering her his belly to rub, which he seldom does with a total stranger. Make that never.

Mom smiled at me warmly from behind her desk. "There, you see? I told you my Benji would be home soon."

I gazed at Boso in silence as Mom's window air conditioner racketed away. Boso gazed back at me, her haunted blue eyes narrowing.

It was dusk by now. I'd moved the Brougham from the garage near Lincoln Center to the one around the corner on Amsterdam where we usually keep it. I'd removed my Smith & Wesson from the glove compartment and tucked it into my daypack.

"Boso and I were just having a very interesting conversation about anatomy," Mom added. "Did you know that giraffes and mice have the same exact number of—"

"Nineteen. We have seven. Yeah, I'm fully up to speed on that."

"I totally thought you were kidding me," Boso said, her words tumbling out nervously. "When you told me your mother used to be a pole dancer, I mean. And Rita's *gorgeous*. I'd give anything to be that tall. I felt like a danged troll standing next to her."

I looked at Mom. "And Rita is . . . ?"

"Spending quality time with Myron."

I sat in one of the chairs opposite Mom's desk. I looked at Miss Jonquil Beausoleil of Ruston, Louisiana. Looked at her gym bag that was on the floor next to the sofa. Looked back up at her and said, "What are you doing here?"

"Hello to you, too. How's your apple juice?"

"What are you doing here?" I repeated, louder this time.

"You gave me your card," she said, stroking Gus's belly. "Remember?"

"I do remember. I also remember that you tore it into pieces. So let's try it one more time. What are you doing here?"

"I got scared when I heard that somebody shot Morrie," she confessed, swallowing.

"Where were you when it happened?"

"At the big Ralph Lauren store on Madison Avenue. Two of the sales clerks were talking about it. It was all over the Internet, I guess. And I thought, like, what if I'm next?"

"Why would you be next?"

"I don't *know*, okay? But right after it happened one of Little Joe's flunkies, Paulie, called me on the disposable cell they gave me and he was, like, 'Why are you so late getting back from the gym?' When I told him I was at the Ralph Lauren store he said, 'You didn't tell us you were going there.' And I was, like,

'What am I, a prisoner?' And he was, like, 'Stay put. I'm sending someone to pick you up.' I told him I'd just catch a cab."

"Then what did you do?"

"Came straight here."

"Say hello to our new client, Bunny," Mom said brightly.

"How did you get here?"

"Benji, why are you asking me so many—?"

"Did you take a cab?"

"I walked. Across Central Park, then up Central Park West to 103rd."

"That's a mighty long walk in this heat."

"I needed the exercise. You kidnapped me before I could get to the gym, remember? Besides, we don't call this hot where I come from. We call it picnic weather."

"What did you do with your cell phone?"

"Tossed it in a trash can on Madison Avenue right away."

"Smart girl," Mom said approvingly.

"Don't use one of our landlines to call anyone. Don't send off any e-mails either. You've disappeared, got it? Mom, has anyone stopped by with a delivery since she got here? A messenger service, FedEx . . . ?"

Mom shook her head. "The only other person who knows she's here is Rita."

"Good." I got up and began pacing around the office, my wheels spinning. "It so happens, Boso, that a whole lot of people want to know where you are. If we're going to stick our necks out for you then we have to know everything."

She leveled her gaze at me. "Ask me anything you want to know."

"Did you shoot Morrie Frankel?"

"No way," she answered angrily. "Why would I?"

"Because you were furious with him. You told me you'd make him sorry. That could be construed as a threat."

She sat there stroking Gus, who gazed up at her adoringly with his urine-colored eyes. "Sure, I was mad. But it's not like I'd shoot a guy just for lying to me."

"Boso makes a good point there, Bunny," Mom said. "If we went around shooting every man who lied to us then there wouldn't be any of you left on the planet."

"Besides, I don't even have a gun. Don't like them."

I snatched her gym bag from the floor. The one that was so heavy and clunky. I unzipped it.

"Hey, what are you doing?"

There was a change of clothes inside. A cropped tank top, yellow. A pair of spandex shorts, blue. And a thong, pink. Underneath the clothes lay a blue metal disc with handles. It was about the size of a dinner plate. The words SMART BELLS LITE were stamped on it.

"I use that for my ab crunches," Boso said defensively. "What'd you think—that it was a gun?"

"Where were you at the time of the shooting?"

"At the Ralph Lauren store. I just told you."

"Their security cams will clear you. *If* you're telling us the truth, that is. Did you buy anything while you were there?"

Boso shook her blond head.

"Do you still have the credit cards they gave you?"

"No, I tossed them when I tossed the phone," she replied, glaring at me. "And you want to know something? I'm starting to think I made a real mistake coming here. You said you'd help me. You're not. You're just being a butthead."

I sat back down, lacing my hands behind my head. "Maybe that's because I've just spent a fun-filled hour at twenty-six Federal Plaza being grilled by a U.S. attorney, an FBI agent and a lieutenant from the NYPD's Organized Crime task force. Maybe it's because at this exact minute they are in the process of raiding the Crown Towers."

Boso let out a horrified gasp. "No way . . ."

"Yes way. Every single person who calls the Crown Towers home is being escorted out in handcuffs. Every single person except for *you*. If you'd gone home this afternoon they would be arresting you right about now for being an accessory to credit card fraud and identity theft. Those are federal crimes, in case you're keeping score. Except you didn't go home. Which is lucky for you but also, well, not so lucky. Do you have any idea how this will look to the Minettas?"

Her eyes widened with alarm. "Like I ratted them out or something?"

"Or something."

"Oh, shit . . ."

"Meanwhile, the NYPD's top homicide investigator is looking for you in connection with Morrie's shooting. You are what's known as a person of interest. You are also what's known as serious bad news. What we ought to do is turn you over to him right this second."

"So why don't you?" she demanded.

"I'm thinking about it."

"Hey, don't knock yourself out on my account."

"Hey, don't worry. I won't."

"Can I get you another water, dear?" Mom offered her.

"No, I'm fine, Mrs. Golden."

"Make it Abby, okay?" She eyed Boso appraisingly. "You must work out eighteen hours a day. My body never looked like yours. Not even in my heyday."

"I spend a lot of time at it," Boso acknowledged. "Last winter I was cheerleading *and* competing in gymnastics."

"So you're a gymnast, too?"

"Well, yeah." Boso sprang to her feet and proceeded to bend all the way over backward until her hands touched the floor behind her. Then she lifted her feet up into a full handstand and walked around Mom's office on her hands, nimble as can be, before she lowered herself back down to the floor with her legs stretched wa-a-ay out in a perfect split. "The webcam pervs just love this pose," she said.

"I'm sure they do," Mom said.

"Is it okay if I use your bathroom?"

"Of course, dear. It's right through that door."

Boso leaped back up onto her feet and went into the bathroom, closing the door behind her.

"What do you think, Mom?"

"I don't smell killer on her," she answered quietly. "Just a little girl with big dreams who got caught in the crossfire. You?"

"Same. I'm thinking we should keep her here tonight. She can sleep upstairs in my place. I'll bunk on the sofa down here. And talk to Legs in the morning. See if I can cut her a deal."

"Legs will come through for you if he can. But he can't help you if it's a federal rap."

"I know that. We'll really have to thread the needle to keep her out of jail."

"It may not be possible, Bunny."

"I know that, too."

Boso returned from the bathroom. "So why don't you?" she demanded, raising her stubborn chin at me.

"Why don't I what?"

"Call the law on me."

"You're our client. We look out for our clients."

She seemed taken aback. "I . . . can't pay you, you know."

"Not a problem," Mom assured her. "That happens sometimes. Have you had dinner?"

She hadn't. None of us had.

"I'll have Diego prepare trays for us," Mom said, reaching for her phone to call downstairs. "I think tonight's special is chicken à la king."

Boso shuddered. "I don't eat anything that's ever had eyeballs."

"How about a salad then?"

"Can I have a kale smoothie?"

"I'll get you one across the street at Lucy Juicy."

"You don't have to do that, Benji. I'll go get it."

"Not a chance. The NYPD is looking for you. The Feds are looking for you. And before the evening is over the entire Minetta crime family will be looking for you. You're not going anywhere."

It was still stiflingly hot outside. The muggy evening air

smelled strongly of rotten eggs. I took my time fetching Boso's kale smoothie. I wanted to see if anyone was watching our building. I moseyed my way up and down both sides of the block with my hands buried in the pockets of my shorts, my eyes flicking this way and that. I saw no surveillance vans parked anywhere. No one sitting in a parked car. No one hanging out on the sidewalk. No Con Ed crews were digging up the street. No UPS trucks were making any late deliveries. Nobody was doing much of anything. Just sweating.

By the time I got back upstairs with our food, Mom and Boso were parked in front of the TV in Mom's office watching the live coverage of Operation Yum-Yum on NY1. The Feds were putting on an impressive made-for-TV event, complete with a camera-ready perp walk of young guys in handcuffs being led out the front door of the Crown Towers.

"There's Little Joe!" Boso cried out, pointing at a defiant-looking weasel wearing a Hawaiian shirt and way too much product in his wavy black hair. "And that's Petey!" The resident webmaster was not at all defiant looking. Geeky was more like it. The rest of them were an assortment of smirking pinheads in tank tops. They were followed out the door by the webcam girls in their tight, revealing clothing. Absolutely none of them were smirking. They looked frightened and terribly, terribly young. "There's *Luze*. . . . And Chantarelle, and—and Christa and Little Mutt . . ."

Mom said, "Why do they call her Little—?"

"Mom, please don't go there. I really don't want to know."

"Oh, my God . . ." Boso began to weep as she sat there. She seemed genuinely blown away by the harsh reality of seeing her girlfriends being led off in handcuffs. "I am *so* screwed right now."

I didn't spot Sue Herrera or Jack Dytman at the scene, but I sure did see a lot of U.S. Attorney Gino Cimoli, which didn't surprise me one bit. The man had glory-grabber written all over him. "Online pornography may not be against the law," he proclaimed for the news cameras in a booming voice. "But credit card fraud is. Identity theft is. Racketeering is. And it will not be tolerated by the U.S. Department of Justice."

"What'll happen now?" Boso asked me in a tiny voice as I unwrapped our dinners on Mom's desk. "What'll they do to my friends?"

"There's no such thing as federal night court. They'll be held over for arraignment in the morning."

"You mean they'll have to spend the night in jail?"

"I'm afraid so. Once they post bail in the morning they can go home, although I'm betting the Crown Towers will be locked down. They'll have to find somewhere else to crash."

Boso wiped her eyes, snuffling. "Oh, my God . . ."

"You look a little pale, dear," Mom observed. "Drink your kale smoothie."

"I—I feel sick to my stomach."

Me, I was starved. I sat down at Mom's desk and started in on my chicken à la king special, which came with rice, string beans and a fruit cup. I'd barely taken my first bite when my cell phone rang. I glanced at the screen, got up and took the call in the outer office, shutting Mom's door. "What's up, Cricket?"

"Are you shitting me? You heard about the raid, right?"

"Mom and I were just watching it on TV. Quite some show."

"So what have you got for me, cutie?"

"Cricket, I have no idea what you mean."

"Benji, this is *me,* the girl who knows how to connect the dots. Morrie Frankel was in bed with Joe Minetta. Morrie gets bumped off today, gangland style, and now Little Joe Minetta's harem of teen skanks get paraded out the door of a Staten Island high-rise by the Feds. Give, will you? Where is she?"

"Where is who?"

"Jonquil Beausoleil, the little blond cutie who you were looking for. The one who goes by the screen names of Cassia, Lisa B and Eva E. She wasn't one of the girls who got busted tonight. Wasn't there, period. So where is she?"

"How should I know?"

"Don't you play dumb with me, Benji Golden."

"Cricket, why don't you just forget about her, okay?"

"Why should I?"

"As a favor to me."

"Sure, I can do that," she said easily. "*If* you tell me why I should."

"I don't know anything. I'm not involved in this case anymore. My client's dead, remember? I've moved on."

"Like hell you have. Tell me something that no one else knows. Do that for me and I'll give Jonquil Beausoleil a pass. Although I have to say I'm getting *really* curious now as to why I should. Are the two of you—?"

I hung up on her and went back in Mom's office. Boso was on the sofa sipping her smoothie.

Mom was at her desk tucking into her chicken à la king. "Who was that?"

I sat back down and had another forkful of mine, which for some reason now tasted remarkably like Elmer's Glue. And it was usually such a palate pleaser, too. "Cricket. She never lets me forget that we have a history. As if I could."

Boso raised an eyebrow at me. "Old girlfriend?"

I nodded. "And a very savvy reporter. She wanted to know why you weren't busted tonight with all of the others. And she was positive I'd know where you were."

Her eyes widened. "How did she figure that out?"

"Because she has amazing instincts and great sources."

"What did you tell her, Bunny?"

"That I was off the case."

"Did she believe you?" Boso asked.

"Not a chance. But you know what? Right now Cricket qualifies as the least of your worries." I shoved my uneaten dinner aside and grabbed Boso's weighted gym bag. "You're spending the night with us. You can have my bed."

"Where will you sleep?"

"Right here. That way I can keep on eye on things."

"I'm not kicking you out of your own bed, Benji. I can crash down here."

"Not a good idea. It's too accessible to the street." Not to mention too easy for her to slip out on us and disappear into the night. "Are you ready?"

"I guess so," she said with a shrug of her shoulders. "G'night, Mrs. Golden. Thanks for being such a sweetie."

"Think nothing of it, dear. And my name's Abby, remember? I'll be right downstairs from you if you need anything. Just knock."

We took the stairs and, I'm happy to report, didn't encounter either of the Felchers as we climbed our way past the third floor.

"This is Mom's apartment," I said when we arrived at the fourth floor landing. "And I've got the penthouse." I unlocked my door when we got there.

"Wait, what's up there?" Boso asked, gesturing to the stairs that continued on past my place.

"The roof garden."

Her eyes lit up. "For real?"

"Okay, I may have been overselling it a bit."

"Can I see it? Please?"

We climbed the last flight of stairs. I unlatched the steel door, shoved it open and we went out onto the roof, hearing the traffic down below on Broadway, seeing the many lights in the many windows of the taller apartment buildings that surrounded us.

"It's just your basic tar beach," I said, inhaling its fragrant essence.

"I *love* it up here!" Boso spread her arms wide and twirled around and around just like a little girl. "I can see the sky!"

"We'd better go back inside now. And don't come back up here in the morning, okay? Stay off the roof."

"Why?"

"Because someone may be watching our building."

That scared her in a hurry. "Okay," she responded obediently. "Whatever you say." I led her back downstairs and, frankly, she was a whole lot more excited about the roof than she was about my apartment. Just stood there in the living room looking around with crinkly nosed disapproval. "Dang, this looks like an old lady's place. Where on earth did you get your furniture?"

"From an old lady."

"And what is that smell?"

"Kasha knishes."

"Kasha *what*?"

"Is there anything else you want to get off your chest?"

"Well, yeah. Gus has really bad breath. His teeth need cleaning."

"Duly noted. Anything else?"

"I don't like the way you dress. You look like a skater punk."

"It so happens I was in costume today."

"How do you usually dress?"

"Not that differently, actually. And you can feel free to shut up any time now. There are fresh linens in that cupboard in the hallway. And the bedroom has AC but our wiring is so old that you can't run anything else once it's on. Not even the coffeemaker, okay?"

"I don't drink coffee."

"If you blow a fuse the fuse box is in the kitchen. The spare fuses are—"

"Wait, what's a fuse box?"

"Tell you what. If the power goes out just knock on Mom's door, okay?"

Boso tilted her head at me, studying me curiously. "I asked her about that story you told me. What happened to you when you ran away, I mean. She said it really happened."

"Well, yeah. Did you think I made it up?"

"I wasn't sure. Guys make up all kinds of stories."

"I don't."

She looked at me through her eyelashes. "Can I ask you something personal?"

"Sure, what is it?"

"Do you like me?"

"Sure, I like you."

"Then why aren't you hitting on me right now?"

"You're a client. That would be unprofessional. And *why* is this a topic of conversation?"

"I guess because I don't understand why you're being so nice to me."

"You're in trouble and somebody has to help you. That somebody is me. Besides, I happen to like Farmer John."

"What's he got to do with it?"

"He's in love with you, silly. Double bolt the door after I leave. Don't let anyone in except for me, Mom or Rita. Don't call anyone. And don't answer the phone if it rings. I'll see you in the morning, okay?"

"Wait one sec . . ." She slid neatly, way too neatly, into my arms and hugged me tight. "I just wanted to say thank you. You're a sweet guy. And I—I guess I'm kind of freaked out right now."

I tucked a loose strand of her ponytail behind her ear and gave her my most reassuring smile. "You'll be safe here. Just holler if you need anything."

Mom was busy making up the office sofa with sheets that she'd brought down from her apartment. Gus was busy helping her, which is to say standing on each and every corner that she was trying to tuck into place.

She gave everything a final tug and said, "There we are. All comfy cozy."

Gus certainly was. He stretched right out, his tail swishing.

"You didn't have to go to all of this trouble, Mom."

"Nonsense. I won't have you wrapped in a ratty old blanket like a homeless person." She hesitated, arching an eyebrow at me. "She's cute."

"She's a kid. Barely eighteen."

"Seems like a nice girl, too. Not cynical and hard."

"Mom, I'm not planning to tiptoe upstairs in the night. You don't have to worry."

"That's just it. I never have to worry. And that's what worries me."

"Um, okay, you just lost me."

"Ever since Rita took up with Myron you've been all by yourself. You don't date. You don't even look. That place around the corner where the hardware store used to be? There are nice-looking single women in there every night but you won't go near the place. It's not natural, Bunny. A healthy young man like you should be having sex at least three times a week."

"Actually, a healthy young man like me should be having sex at least three times a *night*. But let's not quibble. It's too hot. I'm fine, Mom. Really, I am. Now why don't you go up and get some sleep, okay?"

She let out a sigh. "Okay, fine. I'll mind my own business." And went upstairs to bed.

I went downstairs to make sure our street door was locked. Sometimes it doesn't catch if we've buzzed someone in. Then I went back up, bolting the office door behind me. I had a spare toothbrush in my daypack along with my Chief's Special. I brushed my teeth, turned off all the lights and, gun in hand, looked out the wraparound windows at our second-floor view of Broadway and West 103rd. Wilted people were still oozing along the sidewalk in the late night heat. Cabs and buses were coming and going. But I saw no one staked out in a parked car. No one lounging in a doorway. Nothing seemed out of the ordinary.

I peeled off my clothes and slid between the sheets, keeping my gun close at hand. Gus padded around on top of me until he got good and settled on my left hip, grateful for an all-night visitor. I lay there, acutely aware that if I went upstairs right now Jonquil Beausoleil might be grateful for an all-night visitor, too. Also acutely aware that I wasn't going anywhere. There are times when I wish I were some other guy. A guy who'd just march up those stairs, shtup the hell out of that emotionally scarred little hottie for seven hours straight and not think a thing of it. But I'm not some other guy. So I lay there in the semidarkness of the streetlights, eyes wide open, ears tuned to the rhythm of the traffic outside. It got quieter as the minutes and hours ticked by. The late-night revelers went home to bed from the neighborhood bars and restaurants. Fewer cabs and buses drove by. The subway trains rumbled underneath our building less frequently. But I didn't sleep. I was still wide-awake at 2:00 A.M. when I heard a single set of footsteps on the sidewalk approaching our door and coming to a halt.

Right away, I was on alert.

Our street door doesn't have the world's most secure lock. A seasoned pro can pick it in less than ten seconds.

This one needed less than five.

I heard the door swing open on its rusty hinges and click shut. Then I heard someone coming up the stairs. I jumped out of bed and darted across the office, gun in hand. There's a tall filing cabinet in the outer office right next to the hallway door. I crouched behind it, leveling my Chief's Special at the door when I heard the footsteps stop there. I heard the door handle jiggle. A click as the door was unlocked. Saw a light from the hallway as the door swung open. A hand reached inside. Then a light came on and . . .

It was Rita.

She was standing there in the doorway wearing a skintight silver minidress, high-heeled sandals and a shocked expression. I couldn't blame her. I was standing there in my tighty whities pointing a loaded handgun at her.

"Jesus, Benji! What are you doing?"

"What are *you* doing? It's the middle of the night!"

She closed the door and flung her shoulder bag onto her desk. "I had some work to catch up on. Did the AC in your bedroom crap out again?"

"No, we have an overnight guest. There've been some developments." I noticed now that her smooth, lovely face was etched with strain. "What's happened, Rita?"

She ran her hands through her mane of flaming red hair, kicked off her sandals and padded barefoot into Mom's office, where she flicked on the desk lamp and worked the combination on the big Wells Fargo safe. She opened it and pulled out the bottle of Courvoisier that a satisfied client gave us last Christmas. Found us a couple of glasses in the credenza next to Mom's desk and poured us two stiff jolts while I put on my T-shirt and rumpled madras shorts.

Rita took a sip of hers, then she sat down on my makeshift bed and stretched her incredibly long, incredibly shapely legs out on the coffee table.

"Myron dumped me tonight," she informed me quietly.

"What do you mean, he dumped you?"

"I mean we had a lovely dinner at a French restaurant on First Avenue. Drank a nice bottle of wine. Then strolled back to his place, where he sat me down on the sofa, poured me a large cognac and very politely told me that he didn't see a future for us. He said he was sorry but that he can't afford to invest any more time in a relationship that's not going to yield long-term benefits."

"Is this guy looking for a soul mate or a dependable mutual fund?"

She sipped her cognac in hurt silence, her eyes welling up with tears.

"Would you like me to talk to Myron for you?"

"And tell him what?"

"That he's making a huge mistake and he's going to be sorry for the rest of his life."

Rita mustered a smile. "My little knight in shining armor. Thank you, but Myron is very decisive. If he says it's over then it's over."

"Then in that case, I say good riddance. He obviously didn't cherish you enough to deserve you. Forget about him. Move on."

"Tell me something, will you, little lamb?" Her eyes locked on to mine. "You always know the right thing to say to me. You adore me just the way I am. No one has ever made me happier than you. So why on earth couldn't you be a measly fifteen years older?"

"You'd have to talk to Mom about that. I had no say in the matter."

We sipped our cognacs in guarded silence. Did I find myself staring at those beautiful legs of hers? Yes. Did she notice me staring at them? Oh, yes. Was anything going to happen between us right now on that makeshift bed? Oh, no. That was over and done.

Rita took a deep breath, letting it out slowly. "I'll be okay about Myron. I just really didn't feel like going home. I thought if I came in and got some work done that maybe . . ." She trailed off, frowning at me. "*What* developments?"

"A joint FBI-OCCB task force raided the Crown Towers tonight. They busted everyone in the place. Everyone, that is, except for the person who was our link to the Morrie Frankel case."

"Your little webcam hottie?"

"Boso was conveniently AWOL when the place got raided. The Minettas have got to be thinking she cut a deal behind their back."

Rita peered at me over her glass. "So she's asleep in your bed right now?"

I nodded my head. "Unless she's awake."

"Kindly explain something to me. She's frightened. She's alone. She has *the* most perfect bod you're ever going to run across . . ."

"Second most perfect."

"Seriously, Benji, what on earth are you doing down here?"

"My job."

" 'Your job,' " she repeated doubtfully. "If you say so. Will I be bothering you if I work at my desk for a while?"

"No more than usual. Mom was afraid we were going to lose you, you know."

"Not a chance. Golden Legal Services is stuck with me."

"Good, I'm glad."

"Are you sure about that?"

"I couldn't be more sure."

Rita put the bottle back in the safe, swung the door shut and spun the combination dial. "If anyone tries to get in I'll hear them. I'll lock up when I leave. Sleep tight, little lamb."

She flicked off the desk lamp and closed the door. I got back into bed. Gus padded around until he'd settled himself on my hip again. I lay there. But I didn't sleep. I never sleep.

BY 7:00 A.M. I was out prowling the street outside our office with my Chief's Special tucked in the rear waistband of my madras shorts and a sense of profound uneasiness creeping its way through me. It was already 88 degrees out there, and the steamy morning air smelled like spoiled milk. The weather forecasters were predicting that Day Five of the Heat Wave of the Century would top the 100-degree mark yet again, with the added bonus of a slight chance of thunderstorms.

But it wasn't the weather that was making me uneasy.

Our little stretch of Upper Broadway was already plenty busy. The downtown traffic was heavy and there was a whole lot of honking going on. There always is when it's hot out. Bleary-eyed office workers were trudging their way to the subway. Hakeem, the corner grocer's son, was hosing down the sidewalk. Stavros, the fishmonger, was taking a delivery from a refrigerated truck. Starbucks was hopping. Scotty's diner had cabs lined up outside as drivers stopped to grab the famous breakfast special—a fried egg on a toasted onion bagel. I'd already had mine with two large coffees while I sat at Mom's desk and scanned New York City's three daily newspapers.

Our overnight guest was right there on the front page of the *New York Post* wearing her black velvet thong and her most inviting smile. Semi-revealing photos of Boso and several of the other webcam girls had been assembled into a titillating collage underneath a banner headline that read: "YUM-YUM!" The *Post*'s chief competitor, the *New York Daily News*, had opted to go with a photo of Little Joe Minetta being led out of the Crown Towers in handcuffs with a sniveling expression on his weasely face—and a banner headline reading: "PUSSY GALORE!" The raid was juicy enough to bump the coverage of the great Morrie Frankel's shocking midtown slaying to the inside pages, where I learned nothing I didn't already know—other than that they *had* dimmed the marquee lights on Broadway last night in tribute to his passing. And a number of theatrical luminaries did step up and call him a "legend" and "the last of the great showmen." Leah, I felt, would be pleased. Thanks to *The New York Times*, which had its story about the Crown Towers raid tucked inside on page A-18, I learned that the joint NYPD-FBI task force had also raided three different secure storage facilities not far from the Crown Towers where they'd seized an estimated $4.2 million worth of illegally purchased luxury goods.

Big Joe Minetta, who was not personally targeted by Operation Yum-Yum, had issued a statement late last night through his celebrity lawyer blasting the operation as a "witch hunt" and a "cheap publicity stunt." He vowed to "clear the good names of these honest, hardworking American businessmen and women."

Each and every one of those hardworking American businesswomen was mentioned by name in the news coverage, including Luze Santiago, age twenty, from Camden, New Jersey, and Eleanora Yelmas, age nineteen, from Altoona, Pennsylvania, whose professional name was Little Mutt. There was no mention that one of the webcam girls was still at large. No mention of Boso at all.

Or at least not in the newspapers.

The home page of *crickoshea.com* featured a full-frontal nude photo of Boso from that yacht gallery and a big fat question: "WHERE IS SHE?" "According to my sources," wrote Cricket, "Jonquil Beausoleil, the sweetest of the *sweetgirls* webcam babes, was *not* picked up with the others last night. Jonquil's nickname is Boso. She's eighteen and hails from Ruston, Louisiana. My sources believe she's hiding out from both the law *and* the Minetta crime family. All I can say is: Lotsa luck, cutie."

I'd asked Cricket to forget about her. She hadn't. She'd even managed to come up with Boso's age and place of birth. I wondered how. Just as I wondered how long it would take before the Minettas came looking for her at the offices of Golden Legal Services. On the face of it, they had no reason to suspect she was connected to us in any way. Unless, that is, you stopped to think about the what ifs. As in what if Morrie had told Joe Minetta that it was us who he'd hired to look for her. As in what if the doorman at the Crown Towers, the one who Sue Herrera told me they'd turned, was playing for both sides and had given my license plate number to Joe. As in what if someone in our neighborhood had spotted her entering our building yesterday afternoon and recognized her picture in the papers this morning. As in what if . . . what if . . .

And so I was uneasy.

My eyes took in everything as I waited for the good folks at Lucy Juicy to make Boso a breakfast smoothie. I saw no one watching our building. The street looked okay.

So far.

Smoothie in hand, I strolled back across the street, let myself into the building and grabbed my laptop. Then I rode our temperamental elevator up to the fifth floor, where I tapped on my door. I heard Boso's light, quick footsteps at once. "It's me," I said.

She undid the bolt and flung open the door, wearing her spare tank top and spandex shorts. She looked fresh-faced and healthy. And her mouth was working just fine: "Sweet Jesus, Benji, I'm starting to feel like a danged prisoner. I worked out for an hour and I showered and now I've got nowhere to go and I mean *nothing* to do." She was playing music on my stereo—the digitally remastered original Broadway cast recording of *West Side Story* with Carol Lawrence and Larry Kert. "And, excuse me, but do you ever rock out to anything other than Broadway show tunes from the Fifties?"

"Absolutely. I rock out to Broadway show tunes from the Forties. And good morning to you, too," I said, bolting the door behind me. "Here's your breakfast. It has mango, wheatgrass, coconut water and a bunch of other stuff that's too horrible to say out loud."

Boso popped the lid and took a long, grateful drink. "This is tasty."

"As are you, sweet Cassia." I opened my laptop on the dining table and showed her the nudie collage that was on the front page of the *New York Post*.

She let out a gasp of horror. "That's me! Did they mention me by name?"

"*They* didn't." I tapped at the keyboard and brought up Cricket's Web site. "But *crickoshea.com* has all of your particulars—including that the Minettas are looking for you."

Boso stared at the photo of her naked self on that yacht. "You told me I didn't have to worry about her."

"No, I told you she was the least of your worries. And she is."

She sat down on a dining chair with a sick look on her face. "God, this is just awful. I never expected those photos to be splashed all over the danged Internet. Now *everyone* will see them."

"Hello, they already could."

"Yeah, but they had to go looking for them on a specific site. This is a whole different deal, Benji. It's in your face. *I'm* in your face."

"You mean Farmer John's face, don't you?"

"Well, how'd you like it if someone *you* knew saw your naked junk all over the Internet?"

"I wouldn't. But I'm not like you. No one pays thirty-nine dollars a month just to watch me take a shower. Speaking of which, I need to do that. My cop friend is coming to pick me up soon."

"Am I going with you?"

"You're not going anywhere. Not until I get you a deal. You can stay right here. Or you can hang downstairs in the office with Mom and Rita if you promise to stay away from the windows.

You can't go outside. Not for a walk. Not for any reason. And stay off the roof, got it?"

"But I can see the sky from up there," she protested.

"Just stay off it."

"Benji, I hate this."

"I know you do. But you've gotten yourself into what's known in my trade as a shitstorm. I'm trying to help you. Promise me you'll do what I say."

"Sure, whatever," she said miserably.

I heard footsteps on the stairs now. Someone tapped on my door. I held a finger to my lips and went to it, pulling my Smith & Wesson from my waistband. I checked the peephole. It was Mom.

"Everything good?" I called to her.

"Good as Golden," she replied. A quaint old family expression of ours.

I unbolted the door and let her in. "I was just going to jump in the shower. Would you mind entertaining our guest?"

"I'd be delighted." Her dark eyes twinkled at Boso. "You, young lady, are quite the celebrity this morning. Why don't you come down to the office with me? I'll tell you all about the night Mickey Rourke tried to stuff *seventeen* one-hundred-dollar bills in my G-string."

"Okay, Abby." Boso frowned at her. "Who's Mickey Rourke?"

Mom's face dropped. "God, I'm old."

I closed the door behind them. Boso was a tidy guest, I'll give her that. She'd made the bed. Stowed her things away in her gym bag. Left the kitchen spotless. But there were traces of her all over my bathroom. She'd used my hairbrush—several of her long blond hairs were caught in it. Her wet towel was draped over the shower curtain rod. She'd found a new toothbrush in the medicine chest and used it. When I went to brush my own teeth I discovered an unexpected touch of domesticity—she'd already put toothpaste on my brush for me.

I showered and shaved and put on an unpressed blue oxford button-down, my very best pair of four-year-old madras shorts from the Gap and my white Jack Purcells. It was nearly nine o'clock by the time I got downstairs. Mom and Boso were yucking it up in Mom's office with the AC making a racket and the Ramones, another of Mom's favorite bands, rock-rock-rocking away.

"Ah, here's my boy," Mom exclaimed. "Doesn't he clean up nicely?"

"He does," Boso agreed. "He's kind of cute, you know."

"Believe me, I do."

"Mom, where's Rita?"

"On her way. She just phoned."

"Listen, I want you to hold on to this." I handed her my Smith & Wesson.

Mom studied my face carefully. She doesn't like guns, but she knows when I'm not fooling around. "All right," she said, tucking it into the top drawer of her desk.

"I'll let you know just as soon as I have some news," I said to Boso. "Stay put and stay away from those windows, okay?"

"Sweet Jesus, would you *please* stop saying that? You're scaring me!"

"Good."

"OKAY, WHERE IS SHE?"

"Where is who?"

"Jonquil Beausoleil," Legs said as we tore our way down Broadway in his Crown Vic. "The Feds have a warrant out for her arrest. They're looking everywhere for her. Where is she?"

"How would I know?"

He shot a narrow look at me from across the seat. "So you're going to sit here in my automobile and lie to me?"

"Legs, I don't know where she is."

"Damn, you really are going to sit here and lie to me."

"What makes you think I'm lying?"

"Because I know you, little bud. And if you don't tell me where she is I swear I'll arrest you."

"For what?"

"Aiding, abetting, and being a total pain in the ass."

"And here I thought we were going to have fun working this case together."

"We're *not* working this case together."

"Where are we headed anyhow?"

"Tarzan and Jane's place in Soho. Are you going to tell me where that girl is or do I have to throw you in jail?"

"Don't be silly. You won't do that."

"Yeah, I will."

"No, you won't. You can't. Mom would never forgive you." I gazed out the window at all of the limp, sweaty people who were plodding slowly along in the suffocating heat. They looked as if they were ready to melt into puddles right there on the sidewalk.

"Cricket blasted Boso all over her Web site this morning. She knows her particulars. Knows that she's on the lam from the Minettas. How does she know that? Who's her source?"

"Not me." Legs veered around a cab that had stopped to pick up a fare. "I didn't talk to her."

"So who did?"

"You want me to guess?"

"Go for it."

"Cimoli."

"Cimoli." I nodded my head. "He's a pub slut. He has a big mouth. And he's a fat boy."

"What's his weight got to do with it?"

"Cricket's an amazing flirt when she needs to be."

"Still, the fat boy pulled it off," Legs said grudgingly. "That was one major-league bust. Little Joe and his crew are being arraigned this morning. Big Joe's lawyers arranged bail for everyone."

"Including the girls?"

"Hell, yeah. They don't want those girls getting resentful and talkative."

"Hmm . . ."

"Hmm what?"

"The Minettas have to be thinking Boso ratted them out. That girl's in real trouble, Legs. It wouldn't surprise me if I do hear from her. She and I have a bond, after all."

"Bond? What bond?"

"It's personal. What would you tell her if you were me? Speaking hypothetically."

"Speaking hypothetically? I'd tell her to cut a deal with the

Feds. They can put her in protective custody so she'll be safe from the Minettas. Out there on her own she hasn't got a chance."

"Makes sense. Except I don't trust Cimoli."

"I don't either," he conceded as he steered us around Columbus Circle and down Broadway toward Times Square. "And Dytman I don't know. But Sue's okay. And she's got their ear. Do you want me to feel her out? I can find out what they're in a position to offer if the girl turns herself in. You can relay their offer to her."

"If I hear from her, you mean."

"Right. If you hear from her." He glanced over at me. "What's this 'bond' you two share?"

"It's personal, like I said. Just leave it alone, okay?"

"Not okay. Tell me. Or I won't talk to Sue."

"Fine, if you insist. We're both rape victims."

His face fell. "Oh . . ."

"Are you happy now?"

"Not so much."

"I told you to leave it alone." I looked over at him. He had dark circles under his eyes. Probably worked straight through the night. "Did you get anything off the Navigator?"

Legs shook his head. "It was wiped a hundred percent clean of prints—doors, windows, steering wheel, everything. And nothing was left behind. We're still searching the carpet fibers but so far it's a big zero. And the murder weapon's a virgin. The rifling patterns on the bullets that killed Frankel don't match any we've seen before." He honked impatiently at a delivery van in front of us. "We've studied every piece of 42nd Street camera footage we could get our hands on. The Homeland Security

CCTV footage, the security cams from the College of Optometry and Banco do Brasil across the street. Also anything and everything that the tourists and bystanders have handed in. We must have images from fifty different angles."

"And . . . ?"

"Those damned tinted windows shielded the wheelman completely," Legs answered wearily. "We don't have so much as one good look at him. He could be anybody."

"What about the shooter?"

"The best picture we have is this . . ." He pulled a scanner shot out of a folder on the seat between us. "A tourist from Clinton, Iowa, took it."

It was a photo of the shooter getting back into the Navigator after pumping three shots into Morrie. The shooter wore a pair of latex gloves over what appeared to be fairly small hands. No facial features were revealed at all, not with those big sunglasses and that hoody pulled down low. The hoody was baggy and oversized. So were the sweatpants. At the time of the shooting I'd gotten the impression that the shooter was slimly built. But it was hard to tell anything definitive from the photo.

"Not much to go on, is it?"

"No, it's not," Legs grunted, his jaw muscles clenching as he maneuvered us through Times Square traffic.

I studied the picture some more. "Your techies can estimate a person's height based on the height of the vehicle, can't they?"

"They're working on it, but the shooter's crouched. They can only ballpark it within two or three inches."

"Did the CCTV cameras follow the Navigator after it fled the scene?"

Legs nodded. "It went down Fifth Avenue until it made a right onto West 37th Street."

"A right? I thought you said you flagged it going through the Queens-Midtown Tunnel a half hour after the shooting."

"We did."

"But the tunnel's in the other direction. He should have made a left on West 38th."

"I know."

"So why did he make a right on West 37th?"

"I don't know. And, guess what, there are no CCTV cameras on West 37th. It's not heavily populated. Mostly fashion wholesalers. We're fanned out all over the block at this very minute looking for security cams, but we haven't found any yet."

"What about Sixth Avenue? Did the CCTV cameras pick it up there?"

"Still looking," he answered, getting an edge to his voice.

I thought this over as we went barreling past Macy's and Herald Square. "Let's see, so far you have no way to ID the perps, you have no trace evidence, nothing from ballistics and you lost track of the Navigator after it turned off Fifth Avenue in the *opposite* direction of the tunnel. Sounds to me like you've got shit."

"I've got shit," he conceded sourly. "Thanks for pointing that out."

"No prob. That's what I'm here for, partner."

"And I'm *not* your damned partner."

CHAPTER NINE

THE WORLD'S MOST FAMOUS loincloth boy and his fairy princess lived in a loft on West Broadway. Their building wasn't hard to find. It was the one that had all of the TV camera crews, paparazzi and celebrity gawkers crowded on the sidewalk outside waiting for the golden twosome to poke their precious noses out. A cop in uniform was trying to keep the sidewalk clear so that shoppers could make it inside of the high-end designer lighting store that was downstairs.

Legs parked his sedan in a no parking zone directly across the street. Legs can leave his car wherever he chooses. It's really fun to drive around town with a homicide detective.

As we were getting out of the car my cell rang. I glanced at the screen. I took the call. "Hello, Leah. How may I help you?"

"I don't think anyone can do that, Benji," she answered forlornly.

Legs leaned against the car and made a call of his own. To Sue Herrera, I was hoping.

"They dimmed the lights for Morrie last evening," I pointed

out. "And that was very respectful coverage in this morning's *Times*, didn't you think?"

Leah didn't seem to hear that. "I got up. I made myself some toast. I rode the bus here same as I do every day. But I'm all by myself, Benji. And the manager gave me the fish eye in the lobby when I got here. Morrie was a deadbeat tenant, you know. I'll bet that man knocks on our door today and tells me I've got seventy-two hours to pay up or clear out. I—I'll have to figure out what to do with Morrie's collection."

"What collection, Leah?"

"His memorabilia. Morrie had thousands of backstage photographs and Playbills. He had files on every show he produced. He saved everything. Someone will want to preserve it, don't you think?"

"Yes, I do. I still know some folks at the NYU drama school. Let me know if you want me to call them for you."

"Thank you, I will. I'm sorry if I'm bothering you. . . ."

"You're not."

"But I was sitting here and I suddenly realized that the phone had stopped ringing. The obituary writers are done, and now no one else is calling."

"Like who?"

"Like Morrie's friends. Like his fellow producers. Like any of the hundreds and hundreds of people who he personally gave successful careers to over the years. Not one of them has called me to offer their condolences or to ask me if there's going to be a memorial service. You'd think there would be one, wouldn't you? With performers singing his favorite songs from his biggest hit shows? A Broadway giant has passed, Benji, and *no one* has called. I knew he wasn't exactly liked, but that man gave his life to the theater and it turns out that not one person gave a damn about him."

"That's not true, Leah. You did."

"You're right, I did," she said. "And I feel awful about this mess that he left behind. I saw the way that poor girl got blasted all over *crickoshea.com* this morning. She's just a young actress who got sucked into one of Morrie's crazy scams. And now it sounds like Joe Minetta's gorillas are out to get her."

"They won't. She's in safe hands."

"You know this for a fact, Benji?"

"I do. You have my personal assurance that she's okay."

She let out a sigh of relief. "Well, I'm glad to at least hear that."

Legs had finished with his call and stood there waiting for me now, his right knee jiggling, jiggling.

"Leah, I'm sorry but I have to go now."

"Yes, of course."

"Call me any time. And take care of yourself, okay?" I rang off and Legs and I started across the street. "That was Morrie's assistant. She's feeling kind of lost."

"And so she called you? I swear, little bud, sometimes I think you missed your true calling. You should have gone to Yeshiva and been a rabbi. Or, better yet, converted and become a priest."

"Bite me."

"Hey, that's no way for a man of the cloth to talk, padre."

We elbowed our way through the media horde and buzzed Matthew and Hannah's loft. Legs had phoned ahead. They were expecting us. We were buzzed in. Climbed a cast-iron staircase to the second floor, where a big steel door opened and a tall, slim young woman in a Roadrunner T-shirt and jeans waited to greet us, juggling two cell phones, an iPad and a clipboard. Both cells were ringing.

"I'm Rachel, Matthew and Hannah's personal assistant," she informed us in a rushed voice. "Please follow me."

Rachel led us into a raw industrial space that had a soaring twenty-foot ceiling, exposed brick walls, rough plank flooring and cast-iron support columns. It was an enormous space. Dozens and dozens of tall windows let in the morning sunlight. And floor fans kept it reasonably cool. The décor was so spare that I'm not sure it even qualified as décor. There was an antique pool table. There was a huge Flying A Gasoline neon sign hanging from one wall. And out in the center of the loft space there was a seating area with two leather sofas and a pair of matching chairs grouped around a coffee table. That was where we found the 3-D screen's Tarzan and Jane waiting for us. Way off in another time zone I could make out what appeared to be a stainless-steel restaurant-grade kitchen and a doorway that led to what I imagined were at least a half-dozen bedrooms and baths and a bowling alley.

"Matthew . . . ?! Hannah . . . ?!" Rachel's voice was raised to a polite roar because "Tangled Up in Blue" from Bob Dylan's landmark 1975 album *Blood on the Tracks* was cranked up to 11 on the loft's sound system. "Meet Lieutenant Diamond of the NYPD and Ben Golden of Golden Legal Services!"

Matthew Puntigam reached for a remote and turned the music down. "Have a seat, why don't you?" he said off-handedly. "I was just listening to this fellow called Bob Dylan. Know him?"

"Not personally, no," Legs said as we sat down.

Hannah Lane said nothing. Just smiled at us. She seemed to be in an ethereal daze. Or stoned. Possibly both.

"Know his music, I meant," Matthew said. "I envy the way he sings. It just flows right out of him. So natural. So *him*. It's not a quote-unquote good voice. But *I* think the fucker actually pulls it off. Perhaps that's just me."

"Not exactly," I said. "Pretty much everyone on the planet who has ears has felt that way for the past fifty years."

Matthew furrowed his heavy shelf of brow at me—his patented Me Tarzan frown. My response had thrown him. He was twenty-three. He had been a huge movie star for four years. He was accustomed to believing that every word that came rolling out of his piehole was a genuinely original pearl of wisdom. "You were at Zoot Alors the other night with that Cricket O'Shea person, weren't you?"

"Yes, I was."

"Thought so. I'm very good with faces. It's a talent of mine."

"Nice little place you have here," Legs observed, gazing around.

"Isn't it? Used to be a shirt factory. They made actual shirts here."

"I just like having the space," Hannah said in her soft, trembly voice. "New York is so *crowded*."

The coffee table consisted of a slab of glass set atop an old leather steamer trunk decorated with decals from bygone luxury liners and European hotels. Matthew reached over to it for a blue box of Gitanes, the French cigarettes. He lit one with a kitchen match and inhaled it deeply, letting the smoke out through his flaring nostrils. I was struck by how practiced his mannerisms seemed. Styling. The man was styling. And, once again, I was struck by how small he was. His brow and jaw gave him such a brutish look on the big screen. But seated here in his arena-sized loft Matthew Puntigam was just a shrimp in a torn T-shirt and linen lounge pants.

Rachel continued to hover there with all of her portable devices. "Can I get either of you a coffee?"

Legs and I both declined.

"There's no coffee in *my* coffee," Matthew said pointedly. "Could you make me another?"

"Absolutely, Matthew," she said, whisking a cup from the coffee table.

"And do you think you could get it *right* this time? Double espresso, two sugars. Is that so hard?"

"No, Matthew." She went trekking off toward the kitchen.

"We can't go out for coffee like normal people do," Hannah informed us morosely. "Can't walk down the street. Can't ride the subway. Those people out there won't let us. They follow us everywhere with their cameras. They're just so *mean*." Hannah was from northern Minnesota and the words that passed between her plump, rosy lips had a slight Canadian lilt to them. "I wish they'd just leave us alone. Why can't they leave us alone?" she wondered, gazing at us with those huge, gorgeous green eyes of hers. Up close and in person, the twenty-two-year-old screen goddess was so slender that she resembled a starved, frail child. She wore a snug-fitting camisole and yoga pants. Her wild mane of strawberry blonde ringlets was piled atop her head, showing off her delicate, swanlike neck. Hannah's milk-white complexion was so flawless that it looked as if her skin had never been exposed to the elements. Not sun, not wind, not rain, not any of them. Nor to life itself. Had she ever fallen off her bike and skinned an elbow? Scratched her leg on a thorny rosebush? It was impossible to imagine.

Legs couldn't stop staring at her. He did keep trying to look away—at Matthew posing there like Belmondo with his cigarette, at the Flying A Gasoline sign, at me—but his eyes kept returning to her. I didn't blame him. It isn't often that you sit so close to a woman as breathtakingly beautiful as Hannah Lane. And yet Matthew was cheating on her. With a man who was old enough to be his father, no less.

"It would be so nice to just be able to go out to Starbucks like normal people do," she said.

"But we can't," Matthew said with a shake of his head. "Not without having our every fart being covered in the *Post*. So we have to do for ourselves."

By "ourselves" he meant Rachel, who returned now with his double espresso, two sugars. She waited anxiously for his royal highness to sample it.

"That's more like it," he said gruffly when he had.

"Can I get you folks anything else?"

"No, we're fine, Rachel," Hannah said. "Thank you."

Matthew didn't thank her. Rude. He was conspicuously rude.

"She's my cousin," Hannah explained as Rachel headed back toward the kitchen. "We'd be lost without her, wouldn't we, Matthew?"

He said nothing to that. He was busy drinking his espresso, smoking his cigarette and studying Legs. "How may we help the NYPD?" he asked him. "You said something on the phone about some questions you have?"

Legs nodded his head. "Very informal ones."

"Should a lawyer-type person be here?"

"That's up to you. If you want to involve your lawyer we can come back later."

"Not necessary. Lawyer-type people are utter vermin."

"Besides, we're happy to help," Hannah assured Legs.

"Excellent," he said, flashing her a smile. "Since the Morrie Frankel investigation is so high profile, I have to ask each and every person who knew Mr. Frankel the same exact thing. It's strictly routine. I've invited Ben to come along because it so happens that he was working for Mr. Frankel. Plus Ben has often been very helpful to the department in the past."

All of which sounded like complete bullshit to me. But they accepted what he said without question.

"What would you like to know, Lieutenant?" Hannah asked.

"Where you were yesterday afternoon at, say, one o'clock."

She blinked at him in surprise. "Is that all? That's easy. I was working with a dance instructor at a studio on Warren Street.

I'm trying to get back in shape now that my ankle has fully healed."

"What do you think will happen to *Wuthering Heights*?" I asked them. "Will it ever open?"

"Of course it will." Matthew stubbed his cigarette out in an antique black ashtray from the Stork Club and promptly lit another. "Why wouldn't it?"

"Well, your producer is dead."

"Producers grow on trees. They'll find us another one."

"Who is 'they'?"

Matthew drank down the last of his espresso. "Panorama, who else?"

"And what about Henderson Lebow? He and Morrie had a bitter falling out. Will he come back to direct it now that Morrie's no longer around?"

"Haven't the slightest idea," Matthew said with a shrug.

"But I really hope he does," Hannah said. "It's Henderson's vision that we're staging."

"Not Morrie Frankel's?" I asked her.

"Morrie was just a money man," Matthew sniffed. "Nothing more."

I found myself looking at Matthew Puntigam in horror. I'd never heard anyone dismiss a man's entire life's work quite so thoughtlessly. Especially a man who'd accomplished as much with his life as Morrie Frankel had. Not that I for one second thought that Matthew had scripted his bilious little epitaph on his own. He was, I felt certain, merely parroting the scorn of the director whom he happened to be shtupping behind Hannah's back. "I paid a call on Mr. Frankel at his hotel shortly before he was murdered," I said to him. "He was screaming at somebody on the phone. That somebody was you. He told me afterward that you were trying to back out of *Wuthering Heights.*"

"Not true at all," Matthew responded calmly. "It was nothing like that. Morrie immediately jumped to the worst possible conclusion and then went totally ballistic. The man could be quite impossible to deal with, you know. I simply told him we're contractually obligated to begin filming *The Son of Tarzan* next May in Tanzania. And that if we don't open *Wuthering Heights* pretty damned soon—say, by the first of October—then we won't be able to stay with it long enough for him to turn a profit."

"So you didn't threaten to back out?"

"Not at all. I was just trying to convey the reality of our situation."

"And whose idea was it for you to convey this reality to him?"

"I don't know what you mean by that, little man."

"My name is Ben."

"Of course it is."

"Did Henderson Lebow suggest you call him? Or was it Ira Gottfried?"

"They both did," Hannah answered.

Matthew shot her an angry scowl.

"Well, they *did*," she said defensively. "At Zoot Alors. They said that Matthew and I needed to . . . what did Henderson call it? 'Stick a firecracker up Morrie's ass.' The show has been stalled for weeks and weeks. Partly because of me and my stupid ankle. But mostly because of money."

"Or lack thereof," Matthew said. "Which is utterly stupid. Ira has been offering to put up the bucks for months. And Henderson desperately wants back in as director. The only reason he's out is because Morrie and he had a personal issue of some sort."

"My thing," Hannah said to us, "was why can't all of you men just set aside your ego bullshit and get along? Morrie was *so* territorial about *Wuthering Heights* that it made no sense. I mean, if Ira's going to make the movie then why not let him help out now so we can get on with it? What's the big deal?"

"You didn't know Mr. Frankel very well, did you?" I said to her.

"As well as I wanted to," she replied. "He was kind of a pig."

Matthew was peering at me. "What are you getting at, little man?"

"The name is still Ben."

"Of course it is."

"He was old school. He believed that a Morrie Frankel Production was his and no one else's."

Matthew continued to peer at me. "You say you worked for him?"

"Briefly."

"As what?"

"My firm provided him with legal services."

"So you're a lawyer-type person?"

"No, I'm a private investigator-type person."

He let out a laugh. "You're joking."

"No, I'm not."

"But you don't look anything like a private detective."

"Who were you expecting, Sam Spade in a torn trench coat?"

"Ben, I have been wanting to play a detective for as long as I can remember. I would love to follow you around some time, see what you do all day. What do you say?"

"Not interested."

"I'd pay you for your time."

"Still not interested."

He stared at me in disbelief. He was Matthew Puntigam. People never said no to him. "Why not?"

"Because I'm liable to lose my temper and mess up your face."

He glanced over at Legs, his brow furrowing. "Is he kidding?"

"Who, Ben? No, he never kids. Doesn't know how to." Legs turned back to Hannah. "How did you get there?"

She looked at him blankly. "Get where?"

"To the dance studio on Warren Street."

"Rachel called a car service for me."

"And you?" he asked Matthew.

Matthew reached for another of his Gitanes and lit it. "What about me?"

"Where were you yesterday at one o'clock?"

"Right here," he said, nodding to himself.

"Was Rachel here?"

"No, she was out running errands or something," he said, nodding to himself again. It was a definite tell. He did it every time he told a lie. And Matthew Puntigam was a truly terrible liar—

especially when you considered that he was one of the three or four most successful actors on the planet. "I was doing my vocal exercises."

"How are your voice lessons going?" I asked him.

"Voice lessons?" He was offended. "I'm not taking *voice lessons*. I'm working with a coach so that I'll have the vocal stamina to carry off eight performances a week," he explained, dragging on his cigarette.

"Is smoking a good idea? If you're concerned about keeping your voice strong, I mean."

"Smoking's a great idea," he assured me. "I want the raspy quality that Dylan has. Because Heathcliff is no public school gent, let me tell you. He's a scruff. He needs to sing like one."

"And does he?"

Matthew gave me his Me Tarzan frown. "What are you getting at?"

"I'm told that Mr. Frankel and Mr. Lebow had a serious conversation about lip-synching you. Which Mr. Frankel was totally against."

"I don't know where you heard that. There's been no talk of lip-synching me," Matthew responded, nodding to himself. "When my fans plunk down their hard-earned bucks to hear me sing, it's *me* they're going to hear, not some prerecorded fakery. My voice is fine. And *Wuthering Heights* is fine as well. As soon as the money thing gets sorted out we'll open and be a huge success. Right, Hannah?"

"Absolutely," she agreed.

"So the two of you intend to stay with the show?"

"Of course we will," Hannah said. "It's our dream."

"It was Morrie Frankel's dream, too."

She shrugged her narrow shoulders. "Morrie's gone now."

Matthew stubbed out his cigarette. "Anything else we can help you with?"

"No, we're all set," Legs said.

"Good. I'll show you out." He got up off the sofa and led us across the vastness of their living space toward the door. It gave me a great deal of personal satisfaction to note that the 3-D screen world's Tarzan was no taller than I was. In fact, he may have even been a half-inch shorter.

"Listen, I want to be straight with you fellows about something," he said to us under his breath. "I wasn't working on my vocal exercises by myself yesterday. I was working with Henderson—at his apartment." Matthew opened the big steel door, glancing back in Hannah's direction. "He's been coaching me privately, which she doesn't know about. And I'd rather she didn't. She'll get *very* upset if she finds out he's spending more time with me than her. Hannah's like that when it comes to directors."

"But Mr. Lebow's no longer directing *Wuthering Heights,*" I pointed out.

"Don't be stupid. Of course he is. He and Morrie were just playing games. They fought like mad, those two, but the reality is that Henderson's still under contract to direct the show. And they would have have kissed and made up just as soon as the financing came through. So he's continued to work with me, and he's been a big, big help." Matthew paused, clearing his throat uneasily. "We're all men here. We can keep this between us, can't we? I wouldn't want Hannah to get the wrong idea."

I raised my chin at him. "You mean the right idea, don't you?"

He glared at me coldly before he closed the steel door in our faces.

"DO YOU WANT to tell me what *that* was just about?"

"What do you mean?"

"I mean I was trying to make nice, remember? *You* were psyched and ready to go Hannibal Lecter on that dude's face." Legs unlocked his car and we got back in. "What got into you?"

"He did. Matthew Puntigam is a self-infatuated, no-talent poseur. He's smug. He's disrespectful. He's running around behind that gorgeous woman's back. And did you *see* how short he is?"

"Can't say I noticed."

"You're kidding, right? Please tell me you're kidding."

The weather had changed while we were inside of Tarzan and Jane's loft. Big gray storm clouds had moved in. The sky was getting dark. The forecast had called for a slight chance of thunderstorms. This looked like more than a slight chance.

"Plus he lied to us straight up. There's no way he'll set foot on a Broadway stage unless they lip-synch him. Trust me, Legs, that midget will never expose himself to the kind of ridicule he'd get."

Legs started up the car and pulled away. "Exactly what kind of ridicule are we talking about?"

"Cricket told me that when he breaks into song he sounds exactly like one of the chipmunks from Alvin and the Chipmunks."

"Which one—Alvin, Simon or Theodore?"

"That's what I wanted to know. She wouldn't tell me. Henderson Lebow is totally okay with the idea of lip-synching him. He thinks they can pull it off. Except there's one mighty huge problem—it'll only work if the public doesn't know what's happening. And they will. There's no way Cricket will sit on a scoop of such magnitude. She'll expose Matthew as a fraud and kill his career."

Legs mulled this over as he steered us to Sixth Avenue and started uptown toward the Village. Lightning crackled across the sky, followed by a rumble of thunder. A few fat raindrops plopped against the windshield. "Sounds to me like Tarzan's got himself caught in a lose-lose situation."

"He totally has. My guess? He'd be thrilled if *Wuthering Heights* bypassed Broadway and went straight to the big screen, where lip-synching is considered perfectly acceptable. Hell, Jamie Foxx won an Oscar for playing Ray Charles and he didn't sing one note. My guess? That if Matthew goes to Ira Gottfried and says he wants out, Gottfried would be fine with it. Panorama has no stake in the stage production. And it takes the studio's two biggest screen stars out of circulation for months. Besides, the stage version was strictly Morrie's baby. And there's no way Morrie was going to let Matthew walk. He had him under contract."

"Until, that is, somebody gunned him down. Matthew Puntigam had himself one powerful motive, didn't he?" Legs shook his head in amazement. "Damn, I can already see the headline in the *Post*: 'ME TARZAN, YOU DEAD.'" His cell phone rang now. He glanced down at the screen and took the call. Listened. Listened some more. Then said, "Two o'clock works just fine. You're the goods, Suzy Q." And rang off. "Cimoli's willing to have a conversation with us about Jonquil Beausoleil."

"That's all? Just a conversation?"

"Hey, take what you can get. You did call him a dickwad."

"*You* called him a clown cake."

"Only because he is one."

The sky was getting even darker. It practically looked like nightfall now. As we sped our way past Bleecker Street there was another booming rumble of thunder and then the rain came down—so hard and fast that it felt as if we were going through a car wash. The people who were out in it got thoroughly drenched as they dashed for cover under awnings. The gutters became rushing rivers.

Legs drove on, his windshield wipers on high, paying it no attention. "You think Tarzan's our killer, don't you?"

"I think he's a fraud. All he knows how to do is swing from a vine and grunt. That is *not* my idea of a Broadway star. A Broadway star is supposed to be someone who's larger than life. Someone with huge talent and charisma. Someone who—"

"Oh, God, you're not going to start in on Ethel Merman, are you?"

"Actually, I was steering toward Zero Mostel. But if you want to talk about the one and only Miss Ethel Merman I'd be happy to."

"No, I really, really, don't. I wonder if Henderson Lebow will back his story."

"Of course he will. Matthew's his star and his lover. No way he'll leave him flapping in the breeze."

Legs let out a sigh. "This is going to be one of those cases where everyone's playing us, isn't it? Sue just has to deal with mobsters.

Subtle and complex, they're not. We got stuck with show business people. They're devious. They're smart."

"I wouldn't call Matthew smart," I said as the rain continued to pound down on the roof of the car. "But he is devious."

"What's *her* deal? Hannah, I mean. She comes across as barely with it. You've spent more time around actors than I have. Is she as spacy and dim as she seems?"

"I think she's adopted a persona that works well for her. Someone who exists on a higher astral plane than the rest of us grubby mortals. But you don't get to where she is by being an airhead or a pushover. Trust me, underneath that perfect skin there's somebody focused and driven. Hannah knows how to look out for herself. But she sure has lousy taste in men."

"Do we know that for a fact?"

"Meaning what?"

"Maybe she's got herself a slice on the side, too," Legs suggested.

"Maybe she does," I said, mulling that over.

The rain was starting to let up by the time we'd made it to midtown, those dark, menacing clouds disappearing just as quickly as they'd arrived. The hazy sun broke out again. Steam began to rise off the wet pavement. I rolled down my window but the air felt no cooler or fresher. The Heat Wave of the Century was still very much with us.

Our destination was the shmancy Carlyle Hotel on Madison Avenue and East 76th Street. Or, to be more precise, the shmancy sixteen-story Carlyle House apartments that adjoins the hotel, which has its own entrance on East 77th Street, its own narrow lobby and its own doormen. One of those doormen called upstairs for us on the house phone, then directed us to the elevator.

We got in and rode up to the penthouse, where the elevator door opened directly into the foyer of an English baronial estate, complete with suits of armor flanking the elevator and life-sized paintings of medieval royals lining the paneled walls. The foyer opened into an elegant living room that had floor-to-ceiling bookcases, a fireplace and a grand piano. A sofa and chairs covered in plush burgundy velvet were arranged before the fireplace. On the mantel sat the three Tony Awards that Henderson Lebow had won so far in his illustrious theatrical career.

"Greetings, gentlemen!" The trim and fit director strode toward us with a broad smile on his tanned face. He wore a lilac Izod shirt with the collar turned up just so, neatly pressed white slacks and a pair of UGG rubber-soled slip-ons. The man was meticulously buffed and manicured. Not a glossy black hair out of place. The more I looked at him the more convinced I was that he'd had some work done on his face. The skin was drawn just a bit too tight for a man who was well into his fifties. "Please join us, won't you?"

Seated in one of the chairs was the gaunt, ascetic Man in Black, Ira Gottfried, who acknowledged us with a slight nod of his ponytailed head but otherwise remained still and silent. The world's wealthiest and most powerful entertainment mogul wore the same outfit he'd been wearing the other night at Zoot Alors—a black silk shirt, black jeans, black suede Puma Classics. Which isn't to say that he had on the same exact clothes. Supposedly, he had a closet full of identical black shirts, jeans and Pumas.

"I've ordered us a light lunch," Henderson said, gesturing

toward a pair of room service carts that were tucked discreetly in the corner of the room. "I thought we could eat while we answer your questions, Lieutenant. I take it you haven't caught Morrie's killers yet."

"No, sir. Not yet. But we will."

"Please help yourselves."

There was a platter of sliced roast chicken breast, another of sliced cucumbers, tomatoes and avocados. A basket of breads and rolls. A bowl of fresh fruit salad. A pitcher of iced tea.

Legs and I filled up our plates. Henderson limited himself to a small portion of fruit salad. Ira didn't join us. Possibly he subsisted on grubs and tree bark.

"I want to assure you that this is an informal conversation," Legs said after we'd settled ourselves on the sofa with our food. "Strictly routine questions."

"And yet you brought your bodyguard along." Henderson's eyes twinkled at me he sat in a chair facing us. "Smile, Ben. That was a joke."

Ira didn't smile. Just sat there and listened, his hands folded together before him, index fingers forming a steeple for his chin to rest on. The man gave the impression of being some sort of wise and mystical swami. You'd never guess that his chief contribution to humankind had been to provide it with Tarzan in 3-D.

"You may have legal counsel present if you wish," Legs said, munching on the sandwich he'd made for himself. "We've just spoken with Matthew Puntigam and Hannah Lane. They declined counsel. But the choice is yours."

Henderson speared a piece of mango with his fork and popped

it into his mouth. "What do you think, Ira? Do we dare speak to these cagey ruffians without legal counsel present?"

Ira closed his eyes for a long moment, as if he were in a deep meditative state. "I seem to recall," he said finally, his voice barely more than a whisper, "that one of the people in this room graduated first in his class at Harvard Law School before he accepted an unpaid internship in the Panorama mailroom."

"In other words, we're all yours, Lieutenant." Henderson smiled at Legs warmly. "But only if we get to quiz you, too. Or Ben, I should say."

I took a bite of my sandwich, wondering how it was possible that plain roast chicken on Pullman white bread with sliced cucumber and avocado could taste so amazingly good. "What is it you'd like to know, Mr. Lebow?"

"Why Morrie hired you."

"To find his angel."

"This would be the famously elusive Mr. R. J. Farnell?"

"Yes, sir."

"And did you find him?"

"No, sir, I didn't."

"My turn now," Legs spoke up.

"Ah, yes, your strictly routine questions. Fire away, Lieutenant."

"I've been asked to establish the whereabouts of Mr. Frankel's closest business associates at the time of his shooting. Hannah Lane told us she was at a dance studio on Warren Street, which is easy enough to confirm. Matthew Puntigam told us he was here with you, Mr. Lebow, for a—a . . . what was it he called it, Ben?"

"A coaching session."

Henderson let out a snort. "*Coaching*. So that's what the kids are calling it now? Yes, we were *coaching* here together."

"Can anyone else confirm that?" Legs asked him.

"Of course. The doormen downstairs who let him in. They can also vouch for the time that Matthew left. I assure you that Matthew and I didn't plot anything nefarious. We didn't beg, borrow or steal a Lincoln Navigator. We didn't draw straws to see which one of us was going to dress up like the Unabomber and plug Morrie in the back while the other played getaway driver. We're not the sort of people who do that kind of thing."

"None of us are," Legs said. "Until we are."

Ira Gottfried continued to listen in still silence, his chin resting on his index fingers. He was so quiet I almost forgot he was there. Almost.

"Mr. Lebow, what's the real deal with Matthew's voice?" I asked.

He arched an eyebrow at me. "And this has what to do with Morrie's murder?"

I took a sip of my iced tea. "Maybe nothing. Maybe everything."

"Very well," he said agreeably. "The real deal is that he hasn't got one. Not even after months and months of lessons. Dear Hannah's is lovely. It's by no means professional but it's sweet and genuine. The song arrangements can be crafted to accommodate her. But Matthew possesses what is known as a tin ear. Also an unexpectedly high-pitched range. Honestly? He doesn't sound like brawny Me Tarzan at all. He sounds more like—"

"One of the Chipmunks?"

Henderson stared at me. "Dear God, he *does* sound like one of the Chipmunks."

I leaned forward anxiously. "Which one—Alvin, Simon or Theodore?"

Henderson didn't say. Clearly, I was never, ever going to find out. "Trust me, every time that boy breaks into 'You're Still My Queen' I find myself searching for a ball-peen hammer so as to put him out of his misery."

"That's pretty harsh," I said. "Considering that he's your lover."

"It's not his singing that I'm attracted to." Henderson had another piece of mango. "You have eyes, don't you? Half the planet wants him. And I've got him."

"So does Hannah. Is that a problem?"

"Not for me," he answered breezily. "I can share."

"Is it true that you and Mr. Frankel argued about how to get around Matthew's voice problem?"

"We certainly did. Morrie went berserk when I raised the idea of lip-synching him. He thought it would destroy Broadway forever. I'm more of a pragmatist. I think the audience is there to have a good time and that it's my job to give it to them."

Ira nodded in agreement. "The audience," he put forward sagely, "*wishes* to be entertained."

"My feeling," Henderson went on, "is that if we need to enlist another singer in support of Matthew, then so be it. Because, trust me, he cannot be allowed to go out on that stage and sing. Ben, I'm looking into your eyes and I can see that you don't agree. You're a purist like Morrie was. But we're talking about the theater, Ben, which is nothing more than *illusion*. If the audience wants to believe that Matthew Puntigam is up there on that stage belting his heart out then who are we to deny them their illusion simply because it so happens that the boy can't sing?" Henderson let out a regretful sigh. "But I couldn't bring Morrie around to the idea. He was the most stubborn man I've ever known."

"You went back a lot of years together, didn't you?"

"More years than I care to remember," he acknowledged wistfully. "When I first met him, Morrie was flacking for his horrible bitch of a mom. Also trying to pass for straight. I was doing improv at a dive in the Village called the St. James Infirmary. I still thought I had a future as a performer. A lot of us go through that phase when we're young and foolish, don't we, Ben?"

"Yes, we do."

"But we find our calling eventually. Mine was directing. Yours is peeping through keyholes."

"Actually, there are no keyholes anymore. Hotels use keycards now."

Henderson narrowed his gaze at me. "You said you couldn't find R. J. Farnell. Is Farnell considered a missing person?"

"No, he's considered a nonexistent person. Farnell was a phantom angel. Morrie made him up."

"And then sent you looking for him?" Henderson's face broke into a merry smile. "That old scoundrel was trying to dupe some other backers, wasn't he? Morrie was the last of the riverboat gamblers. Never gave in even when defeat was staring him right in the face. I'm going to miss that fat bastard, you know that? He lied. He cheated. At least half of the words that came out of his mouth were total bullshit. But he believed his own bullshit. And, my God, he loved the theater."

Legs turned to the Man in Black now and said, "Mr. Gottfried, may I ask where you were yesterday at one P.M.?"

"Of course you may," Ira answered softly. "I was in my office on the thirty-seventh floor of the Panorama building on Park Avenue. Am I considered a person of interest, Lieutenant?"

"Well, you do have an interest in this matter."

Ira considered this, his chin continuing to rest on his steepled index fingers. I was beginning to think it was affixed to them with Krazy Glue. "Do I? And what is that?"

"Now that Mr. Frankel's gone you can take over his show."

"It's true, I can. But that was going to happen anyway."

"It was?"

"Oh, absolutely," Ira assured him. "I wanted to be involved from the outset. Matthew and Hannah are my most valuable assets, after all, and I genuinely believe that the film adaptation of *Wuthering Heights* will prove to be the greatest musical in Hollywood history. But Morrie wouldn't take a nickel from me. No matter how dire his financial situation became the answer was always no. Morrie was positive that he'd be surrendering his creative autonomy. Which is in no way true. Ask any of the content providers with whom I've been associated. I don't interfere. But Morrie was a stubborn man, as Henderson said. Consequently, he was going to lose *Wuthering Heights* within the next few weeks. It was inevitable. All I had to do was wait and the show would have been mine."

"So what happens now?" Legs asked him. "Will Panorama take over *Wuthering Heights* and open it this fall?"

Ira Gottfried gazed up at the ceiling, his eyes squinting shut as if he were staring directly into a very bright light. "This is not a question for which there is a simple yes or no answer. There are contractual issues that will have to be resolved. Under common contract law most contracts become void when one of the two parties to the contract dies. We know that there is no Morrie Frankel Productions without Morrie Frankel. We also know that Morrie drafted those contracts himself, and he was nobody's idea of a fool. Therefore, our lawyers will have to sift through the fine print very carefully. It's possible that we will be able to green-light *Wuthering Heights* within a few short days. It's also possible that whoever killed Morrie laid bare a contractual minefield that will effectively delay the staging of *Wuthering Heights* for months, even years."

I went back to work on my sandwich, chewing on it slowly. "Matthew told us that he and Hannah have to start shooting *The Son of Tarzan* in May."

"Correct. The Tarzan franchise is our number-one priority. Principal photography must begin in Tanzania on time. We have an obligation to our shareholders." Ira paused, pursing his thin, pale lips. "Although there is a way to have our cake and eat it, too. Thinking long term, that is to say."

"Which is what?" Legs asked him.

"May I take a crack at this one, Mr. Gottfried?"

Ira studied me curiously. "Very well. The floor is yours, Ben."

"How tight is the script for *The Son of Tarzan*?"

"It's camera ready. Has been for two months."

"Has your casting director found the boy yet?"

"What boy?"

"The boy who'll play Tarzan's son."

He smiled at me thinly. "Yes, she has. In London. I've seen him on video and he's terrific. Our director has already spent a lot of time with him."

"And have they scouted the Tanzania locations?"

"I like how your mind works, Ben. You should come to work for me instead of peeping through keyholes."

"Like I said, there are no more keyholes."

"Our Tanzania locations are all nailed down. And our base camp is staffed and fully operational. It stays that way 365 days a year. We've filmed three mammoth productions there. We are committed to filming a fourth. It's in our interest to keep our production and housing facilities up and running, as well as to keep the local officials well-compensated and compliant."

"In other words, you can ramp up production pretty quickly."

"Our second unit can be there in one week. Our first unit in two weeks. Our stars just need a few days in London for costume fittings and hair."

"And how about the weather?"

"The weather's ideal right now. It's their dry season."

"Okay, *what* are we talking about?" Legs demanded.

"Flipping the projects," I told him. "Matthew and Hannah can go to work right now on *The Son of Tarzan* while all the contractual wrangling over *Wuthering Heights* is being resolved. Then they'll come back and get the stage production up on its feet for next season. And then they'll shoot the film version. Bim-bam-boom. Makes perfect sense. Everyone comes out ahead." I glanced at Henderson. "Except for you, Mr. Lebow. If Matthew and Hannah fly off to Tanzania you'll be left high and dry."

"Who, me? Not a chance," he responded. "I have firm offers to take over the reins of three different shows, each one quite promising in its way. Trust me, I'll be very busy if Matthew and Hannah end up in Tanzania."

"But you'll miss Matthew, won't you?"

"Absolutely. But I'm very good at making new friends. Besides, shelving *Wuthering Heights* until next season might be the very best thing for Matthew. It'll give him more time to get his voice into shape."

"And if he can't?"

"It'll give me more time to figure out how to deal with it."

Legs' right knee was beginning to jiggle. "Will you gents kindly explain something to me? Are you just spitballing right now or is this what's actually going to happen?"

The Man in Black squinted up at the ceiling again for a long moment before he said, "I still believe in *Wuthering Heights*. And I still believe in my stars, despite Matthew's vocal shortcomings."

I said, "It's a sixty-five-million-dollar musical and one of your two stars sings exactly like a cartoon rodent. I wouldn't call that a shortcoming. I'd call it a crisis."

"There is no such thing as a crisis," he lectured me patiently. "A crisis is merely a problem in search of a solution. There is always a solution. You simply have to remain open to receiving it. If you are, then the solution will present itself."

And indeed it had, I reflected, gazing at Ira Gottfried and Henderson Lebow. The murder of Morrie Frankel counted as a very tidy solution to all of their legal and creative problems. They had their ducks in a nice, neat profitable row now. Morrie's death was good for them, good for Matthew, good for everyone. Everyone except for Morrie, that is.

In fact, it was all so damned tidy that I couldn't help wondering if that had been the plan all along.

WE'D MOVED UP in the world.

This time we were in a genuine conference room seated around a table that could accommodate at least two-dozen Very Serious People. There were windows that looked out at the New York County Courthouse. There was a framed photo of the president on the wall. There was an American flag, carpeting. We'd made it to the big time. We even got a chance to watch U.S. Attorney Gino Cimoli strut around the conference room in full peacock mode barking orders into his cell phone. Legs and I sat there in silence with Detective Lieutenant Sue Herrera and Special Agent Jack Dytman, waiting for him to get off the damned phone.

"I heard from the Attorney General personally this morning," Cimoli informed us proudly when he finally got off the damned phone. "He phoned me from D.C. and said two words to me that I'll sure never forget for as long as I live: 'Good job, Gino.'"

I did not, repeat not, point out that the Attorney General had actually said three words to him, not two. After all, I wanted something from this guy. Besides, it was a big day for Cimoli, career-wise. Sue-wise, too, he was obviously hoping. It was pretty clear that his preening was targeted in her direction. It was also pretty clear that Sue was totally oblivious. Her eyes were focused on the screen of her laptop on the table before her. Dytman sat across the table from her, craning his itchy red neck and trying not to claw at it. His heat rash looked even angrier today, if such a thing was possible. I wanted to run out and buy the man some baby powder.

Cimoli plopped his tubby self down in a chair, beaming. "In case you're interested, Lieutenant Diamond, Joe Minetta is being questioned at this very minute by our people about his involvement in the Crown Towers operation."

"Will you be able to charge him with anything?" Legs asked.

"We don't think so. It was Little Joe's baby all of the way. Big Joe is, at most, a material witness. But, believe me, this is not the happiest day of his life. His son is going away for a long, long time." Cimoli gazed across the table at me now. "You wish to have a conversation about Jonquil Beausoleil?"

"Yes, I do. I want her brought in."

"Good, so do I. She's a loose end. I hate loose ends."

Dytman cleared his throat. "Do you know where she is, Ben?"

"Let's say, for the sake of discussion, that I do. What are you people prepared to offer her?"

"For the sake of discussion?" Cimoli said. "That all depends on what she has to offer us."

"Let's say it's game-changing testimony."

"What is it?"

"You'd have to hear that from her."

Cimoli sighed impatiently. "Will it bring down Big Joe? Because it's Big Joe who I really want."

"Like I said, you'd have to hear it from her."

"I'm going to play devil's advocate here," Dytman said, craning his neck. "Why should we go out of our way to cut this one particular webcam girl a deal? We're already flipping all of the other girls. They're more than eager to tell us everything they know. What reason do we have to believe that Miss Beausoleil knows more than they do?"

"How about because she was the only one who happened to be working a side scam with my murder victim?" Legs said. "How about because it was Joe Minetta himself who put her and my murder victim together? That girl is the one and only link between Minetta and Morrie Frankel. It seems to me you'd be mighty interested in what she has to say. I sure am."

"Makes sense to me," Sue Herrera murmured, tapping away at her laptop.

"And there's more," I said. "Her life is currently in danger. Boso was the only girl who wasn't home when you raided the Crown Towers. Really unfortunate timing on her part because now the Minettas have got to be thinking that she ratted them out. They're looking for her."

Cimoli stuck out his lower lip. "I'm going to be candid with you, Ben. That particular argument carries a lot less weight with me. This is a girl who masturbates on camera for a living. She chose this life."

Sue glared across the table at him. "Please tell me you did *not* just say that."

He reddened instantly. "All I meant was—"

"We have a responsibility to protect her," Sue stated firmly. "Whether we like how she earns her money or not."

"I didn't say that we didn't. What I meant was that this girl—"

"Her name is Jonquil Beausoleil. Friends call her Boso. And I'm out of here." I got up and started for the door.

"Wait, where are you going?" Cimoli demanded. "Calm down, will you? Tell him to calm down, Lieutenant Diamond."

"He seems perfectly calm to me," Legs said.

"I was just venting," Cimoli said defensively. "Can't a guy vent? I promise you that if Miss Jonquil Beausoleil is ready to help us then we're ready to help her. You have my word. Now sit back down like a person, will you?"

I sat back down like a person. "What are you prepared to offer her?"

"For now? Protective custody."

"What about immunity from prosecution?"

"Ben, we've got her dead to rights on credit card fraud."

"You didn't answer my question."

"Fine," he huffed. "Immunity's on the table."

"Are you prepared to put her in the Witness Protection Program?"

"Depends on what she's got to say. Don't ask me to promise you anything more right now because I can't. But it's not out of the question *if* she can put Big Joe behind bars. Can she?"

"I honestly don't know. But the only way you'll find out is if you keep her alive."

"What do we know about Miss Beausoleil's whereabouts at the time of the Morrie Frankel shooting?" Dytman asked Legs.

"I'm told she was at the Ralph Lauren store on Madison Avenue. Their security cams will clear her if that's the case. We're checking them."

Cimoli frowned at him. "Who told you that?"

"That would be me," I said.

"So you've been in contact with her?"

"I never said I hadn't been."

"Do you know where she is right now?"

"Yes, I do. Lieutenant Diamond doesn't, but I do."

"I don't believe this shit," Cimoli fumed. "Where is she?"

"I'm not prepared to tell you that yet. I still have one more question I want to ask."

He crossed his arms in front of his chest, glaring at me. "Ask away."

"Who leaked her identity to Cricket O'Shea?"

"What are you looking at me for? I didn't out her."

"Are you sure about that?"

"I'm a sworn officer of the court," Cimoli shot back. "You have got some balls coming here and accusing me of leaking confidential information to a gossip blogger."

"Somebody who has intimate knowledge of the case leaked it to her," Legs pointed out. "Somebody who knew her age, her place of birth. It wasn't me. It wasn't Benji. And it—"

"Hold on a sec . . ." Cimoli glowered at me balefully. "What makes you so sure it wasn't him?"

"Because I know him. I know Sue, too." Legs raised his goateed chin at Cimoli. "But I don't know you."

"You don't know Agent Dytman either. Why are you putting this on me?"

"Because it isn't Agent Dytman's face that I see every time I turn on the TV. You like attention, Cimoli. People who like attention know how to go about getting it—by feeding the beast."

"I didn't leak the Beausoleil girl's name to Cricket O'Shea," Cimoli insisted. "I don't even know the stupid bitch."

"She's not stupid," I said. "And she's not a bitch."

He looked at me in amazement. "I don't get it. Me you disrespect up, down and sideways, yet Cricket O'Shea you're defending?"

"Cricket and I go back a few years. We went to school together."

Cimoli's eyes narrowed. "Is that right? Then I think we know what happened here."

"We do?"

"*You* leaked it to her, obviously."

"Obviously. Except I didn't."

"Obviously," Legs agreed.

"You know what? I've had it up to here with you two assholes!" Cimoli roared. "Who the fuck do you think you are? A poverty-row PI and a hipster homicide detective who's going to be on traffic detail in Ozone Park by nightfall if I have anything to say about it. And, trust me, I do!"

"It seems to me," Dytman put in soothingly, "that the purpose of this meeting is to establish the Beausoleil girl's whereabouts and arrange protective custody for her. We're all on the same side. We all want the same thing. Who cares if Cricket O'Shea has cultivated a source close to our investigation? All she's put out there is the girl's identity. It's not as if the Minettas have any idea where she is."

"Yes, they do . . ." Sue was staring at her laptop's screen.

"What are you talking about?" I asked her.

"Listen to her latest posting: 'Why doesn't some bright boy tighten up his brain and go look for Jonquil Beausoleil at the offices of Golden Legal Services?' "

I felt my stomach clench. "When did Cricket post that?"

"Twenty-five minutes ago. Is that where she is, Benji?"

I nodded my head.

Legs grabbed his cell phone and called it in. "I want that building flooded with men," he said in a hard, commanding voice. "I want bodies surrounding that girl. And the entire intersection secured. I am talking full perimeter protection, got it? And I mean *now*!" He rang off, his jaw muscles clenching. "They'll be there in less than five minutes."

I reached for my own phone and called the office. It was Rita who answered.

"Hey, there," I said, keeping my own voice extremely calm. There are times when I'm grateful for my acting training. "How's our guest doing?"

"That little kitty is a stone freak," Rita answered. "She was getting bored, okay? So she decided to go up to your place for her *second* aerobic workout of the day. She invited me to join her, okay? Let me tell you—within ten minutes I was ready to pass out. She made me feel seventy years old. And I'm in good shape, Benji."

"You're in great shape, Rita. Listen, I don't want to alarm you but they know she's there."

"How . . . ?"

"Cricket found out."

I heard voices from her end now. Male voices. And heard Mom say, "May I help you, gentlemen?"

"Two cops in uniform just barged in here," Rita informed me.

"Good. Legs sent them. And more are on their way. But, listen, just to play it safe you'd better ask for—"

"I'll need to see your photo ID, please," I heard Mom say to them. She is nobody's fool. "Thank you, gentlemen. Allow me to show you the way."

"Rita, tell them to take the stairs. They're liable to get stuck in that damned elevator for three hours."

"Not to worry, little lamb. Abby's way ahead of you. And two plainclothesmen just got here. She's checking their ID, too. It's all good. Boso will be fine."

"Excellent. We'll be there as soon as we can. Oh, hey, Rita? Do me one small favor, will you?"

"Sure, what is it?"

"Keep away from the windows."

Legs and I headed out of the conference room now, moving briskly toward the elevator with the others trailing along behind us. When we got there Legs pushed the button once, twice, three times.

"Why did you do it?" I asked Cimoli as we stood there waiting for the elevator. "Why did you tip Cricket off?"

"I didn't tip her off, you little shit!"

"I don't believe you. And if you call me a little shit again I'm going to slug you."

"I'm all done talking about this, understand? We'll extract the girl from your building and we'll put her in protective custody at an undisclosed location."

"Until Cricket discloses it, you mean."

"Listen, you little—!"

"If you boys don't knock it off," Sue warned us, "I'm going to slug *both* of you."

Legs' phone rang while we were still waiting there for the

elevator. He took the call. Listened. Listened some more. Then rang off and said, "We're too late. We lost her."

I stared at him. "What do you mean we lost her?"

"I mean she's dead."

CHAPTER TEN

ONE OF HER BIG, BLUE EYES—the left one—was gazing directly at me. But that haunted look I'd seen in those eyes was gone now. It had been replaced by a shocked, unblinking stare. And her right eye wasn't even there anymore. The bullet took it out before it went straight through her brain and blew out the back of her head.

She was lying on her back on the steamy tar roof with the hot sun beating down on her. Her arms were spread wide, palms facing the sky. Her tanned legs had splayed rather awkwardly as she fell. It was not her best look. Even so, a crime scene photographer stood over her shooting her from this angle and that for one final pictorial gallery. She was still an object of fascination. The camera loved her.

"I—I told her, stay off the roof," Rita sobbed as Mom and I stood there trying to console her. "After we worked out together in your apartment, I told her do *not* come up here."

"I told her the very same thing, Rita." I put my arms around her and hugged her. She towered over me in her high-heeled sandals. "It's not your fault."

"It's not your fault," Mom echoed softly.

"She kept telling me h-how much she hated being cooped up. She wanted to see the sky."

"She liked to be able to see the sky," I said. "You didn't hear the shot?"

Mom shook her head. "Not over all of our street noise. Not with my AC on."

"I should have stayed there with her," Rita went on. "I shouldn't have left her by herself."

"Rita, you had no way of knowing what would happen."

"Bunny's right, Rita."

"She wasn't a bad kid," Rita sniffled.

"Boso was a good kid," Mom agreed. "And she was smart. She would have made something of herself."

"It's going to be okay, Rita."

Rita breathed in and out raggedly. "No, it's not. It's never going to be okay."

Legs stood over near Boso's body with his face drawn into a tight grimace. All of the bluster had gone out of Gino Cimoli. He looked quite ill. Jack Dytman looked defeated and glum. Sue Herrera just looked pissed off. The roof was crowded with people. An EMS crew was still there. So were a half-dozen cops, the crime scene technicians and the photographer. I wondered if our building's tired old roof could handle so much weight. I wondered if we'd all go crashing down into my apartment below. It wouldn't be such a bad thing, really. The fall might kill me and put me out of my misery.

"What a damned shame," Dytman said, shaking his head.

Legs said, "I swear to God, Cimoli. If I find out that you leaked this to Cricket O'Shea I'll—"

"I didn't," Cimoli insisted. "It wasn't me."

Dytman craned his itchy neck. "What a damned shame."

"If you say that one more time," Sue informed him, "I will throw you off this roof."

"How did the shooter get here so fast?" I asked Legs. "He took her out, what, forty minutes after Cricket posted it on her site?"

"The Minettas wanted this girl gone," Legs said, thumbing his goatee. "My guess? They had shooters who were cruising different parts of the city just waiting to be green-lighted." He looked around at the high-rise apartment buildings that surrounded us on Broadway and on West 103rd Street. "I'm seeing at least eight buildings he could have shot her from. Judging by those entry and exit wounds in her head I'd say he used an M4 sniper rifle. It fires a 5.56 NATO, by way of the .223 Remington. Your standard Special Forces sniper weapon. We can study the angle of the wounds and calculate the trajectory. We'll locate where the shot came from. But I guarantee you he left no trace evidence behind. No shell casing. No fingerprints. No nothing. And no one will remember seeing him. He probably showed up wearing maintenance overalls, his weapon stuffed in a duffel bag. Found himself a nice, quiet hallway window. Or maybe the roof. Was out of there sixty seconds after he took her down. He'll be halfway to Philadelphia or Providence by now—unless he lives in the 'burbs and has a perfectly respectable cover identity." He glanced at me, his knee jiggling, jiggling. "*This* is how a pro operates."

"As opposed to the Morrie Frankel shooting, you mean?"

"Exactly."

"So you think it's a different shooter?"

"I don't think it. I know it." Legs looked over at Rita. She'd burst into tears again. Mom had her arms around her. "How's she doing?"

"Not so good."

"She's lucky that Boso came up here, you know. So's Abby. He would have gone for a window shot if she hadn't. You could have lost more than just her."

"No need to tell me that," I said quietly. I knew perfectly well how close I'd come to losing the two people in the world who I cared about the most.

Legs motioned for me to follow him away from the others. Then he put his hands on my shoulders and said, "Are you okay?"

"Legs, she'd still be alive if I hadn't butted in . She'd be up on credit card fraud charges with the others but she'd be alive. But no, I had to drag her away from that place and play the white knight. I got her killed."

"She got herself killed. You were doing a job. You were paid to find her. You found her. What happened after that isn't on you. Hell, if you're looking for someone to blame then blame me. I knew you were holding out on me when you swore you had no idea where she was. I could have grabbed you by the scruff of the neck and forced the truth out of you."

"So why didn't you?"

"Because your dad taught me that you've got to let a man do things his own way."

"I should have just left her alone."

"You could have," he acknowledged. "But that would have made you a heartless schmuck, and you're not. You're one of the good guys, little bud."

"If I'm one of the good guys then how come my client *and* the girl who he hired me to find are both dead?"

"You tried. Listen to what I'm saying, because if your dad was standing here right now he'd tell you the exact same thing. It didn't work out but you tried. That's all you can do. You drag yourself out of bed every morning and you try. So don't get down on yourself, okay? I'll take over from here. You're all done now."

I stared at him long and hard before I said, "No, I'm not."

IT TOOK ME A WHILE to find her.

First I tried the offices of a couple of big time producers where I knew she liked to hang out during business hours. Then I tried Joe Allen's. Then Bruno Anthony's. Then I began working my way up and down West 45th Street, my eyes flicking this way and that. When I finally spotted her in her pink T-shirt, black jeans and white go-go boots she was bopping her way across Shubert Alley, yapping into one iPhone while she thumbed out a tweet on the other, so absorbed in what she was doing that she didn't even notice me.

Not until I grabbed her by her pale arms and slammed her against the wall of the Booth Theatre.

"Ow, Benji, that hurt! And since when do you like it rough?"

"Who tipped you off?"

"Let me call you back," she said into the phone before she rang off, grinning at me impishly. "I'm liking this new beastie-boy thing you've got going on. You were always a little too gentle, if you want to know the truth."

"Who told you, Cricket?"

"Told me what, cutie?"

"That Boso was hiding out at our office."

"Why are you asking?"

"Because a sniper just shot her right through the eye. It was a professional hit. And it wasn't pretty. And it was *your* fault. You tipped them off. Who told you where she was?"

Cricket gulped. "Jonquil Beausoleil is dead?"

"Severely dead."

"Unfucking real . . ." Her little thumbs promptly went to work on one of her phones. "Hang with me for just one sec because I have *got* to put this out there."

I wrenched both phones from her grasp and hurled them out into the middle of West 45th Street, where they were instantly run over by cabs.

"Benji, that was my whole office!" she cried out.

"Who's your source?"

"You know I can't give up my source. I'd be violating my ethics."

"Cricket, I've known you since we were freshmen together. You don't have any ethics."

"That was an awful thing to say to me, Benji. I know you're upset, but that was just totally mean. Besides, it was a nothing one-liner. A throwaway. I must post a hundred of them a day."

"Yeah? Well, this one got a girl killed. The Minetta family thought she ratted them out. I was trying to get her into protective custody before they could find her. They didn't know where she was. Not until you told them. And then they shot her dead. You don't get it, do you? You're like a kid playing in a sandbox. Except these people aren't playing. They use real ammo. And that girl is really dead. Boso doesn't live here anymore. Tell me who tipped you off."

She shook her head at me. "No can do. Sorry."

"Cricket, I want you to look into my eyes, okay? I want you to understand that I am being totally serious. Tell me who your source is right now or I swear to you that I will devote the rest of my life to making sure that you are toast in this city. You'll have no career. You'll have no friends. You'll be a dead woman walking." My eyes locked on to hers and held them tight. "Tell me who tipped you off. Tell me right fucking now or so help me I'll destroy you. I mean it. Tell me, Cricket."

Cricket told me.

"WHEN YOUR CHILD GETS INTO TROUBLE you don't stop loving him. You love him more, because he needs you more." She was boxing up all of those framed, autographed photos of pimply-faced Morrie standing backstage with Broadway's biggest stars of yesteryear. She was very calm and composed in her trimly cut pale yellow linen dress. She had politely offered me a cup of coffee. I had politely declined. "Charlie is hoping to be a chef someday. He's taking classes. He tries. He really does. But he gets so frustrated by little setbacks. And he's had substance abuse problems. Practically every penny I've made has gone toward trying to keep him out of trouble and clean. He used to tend bar at Barrymore's, that nice little restaurant that was on West 44th Street. Do you remember it?"

"Yes, I do."

"One of his coworkers, a waitress, claimed that Charlie tried to rape her in the kitchen one night after closing. She was going to go to the police. I convinced her to take ten thousand dollars from me instead, and Charlie went into drug rehab. It was all handled very quietly. But your friend Cricket got wind of it because the girl was one of those ambitious young actresses who are always talking to her, hoping to get a nice mention. You know how that works."

"Yes, I do."

"Cricket was planning to run an item about it," Leah said as she removed more of Morrie's photos from the living room wall, leaving one sooty outline after another behind. They'd been hanging there forever. "When she called me for a comment I begged her not to run it. I told her she'd be ruining the life of a decent young man who was trying so very, very hard. Charlie's not a sexual predator, Benji. He's just weak. Cricket agreed to sit on the story *if* I agreed to feed her choice morsels of information that I happen to hear about. I did agree, for Charlie's sake, and she's been holding it over me ever since. If I hear something, I'm supposed to call her—or else. And so I do. I'm the one who told her that Morrie and Henderson got into a lover's quarrel over Matthew Puntigam. She got that story from me after Morrie came to me with tears streaming down his face. And I told her what you said to me on the phone this morning—that Jonquil Beausoleil was in safe hands and that I didn't have to worry about her."

"So you were doing Cricket's legwork for her when you called me."

"Yes, I was," Leah admitted. "And I regret it terribly. But she leaves me no choice, Benji. I had no idea what would happen to that poor girl. She was so young, and none of this was her fault."

"Let's not talk about her, okay? I didn't tell you where she was, Leah. How did Cricket figure out that she was stashed at my place?"

"Because Cricket knows you. She called you a softy and a sap and a number of other names that led me to believe that you two have a history together." Leah looked at me searchingly. "Were you and Cricket romantically involved?"

"Let's not talk about her either. Let's talk about you. Why don't you have a seat, Leah?"

"All right." She sat down on a sofa, her bony, translucent hands folded in her lap. "What would you like to know?"

There was a knock at the door.

"That'll be for me." I went to the door and opened it.

Legs stood there in the hallway with an intense, feral look on his face. "What's so urgent?" he demanded.

"Come on in."

He came on in, clenching and unclenching his jaw.

"Why, good afternoon, Lieutenant," Leah said to him pleasantly.

"I asked the lieutenant to join us, Leah. You don't mind if he's here while we talk, do you?"

"Of course not. Why would I mind? Would you like some coffee, Lieutenant? I can make a fresh pot."

"No, thanks."

"Your timing was excellent, Legs. Leah was just about to tell me why she did it."

"Did what?"

"Kill Morrie."

Leah looked up at me like a panicked animal, then down at the worn rug. "What on earth are you talking about?"

I sat on the sofa across the coffee table from her. Legs stayed on his feet, his ripped, veiny arms folded in front of his chest. "Joe Minetta is a loan shark. He wanted Morrie alive, not dead. Ira Gottfried is a cold-blooded shark, too. But he's also a very patient man. All he had to do was wait for Morrie to implode and then pick up his leavings. He didn't have to hire a hit man to bump him off. But the attack on Morrie wasn't a professional job. My friend Legs here knew that right away. A professional wouldn't have shot Morrie on 42nd Street in broad daylight in front of so many witnesses. No, Morrie's shooting was the work of a small-time lowlife. Someone like, say, your son Charlie."

"I ran his sheet on my way over here," Legs said, leafing through his notepad. "Charles Nelson Shimmel has two priors. One for possession with intent to sell, the other for breaking and entering. He served eighteen months on the B and E."

"Mind you, a good deal of careful planning did go into Morrie's murder," I continued. "And that points to someone with an organized mind. Someone like you, Leah. Morrie's shooter was smallish and on the slim side. That was you in the hoody and sweats, wasn't it? Charlie was behind the wheel. You did it together."

Leah didn't dispute this. Didn't say anything at all. Just sat there on the sofa, calmly and quietly.

"Why did you do it, Leah?"

"Why?" Her lower lip began to quiver. "You're just a kid. You don't know a damned thing about life. You can't possibly understand."

"Help me to understand. I'd really like to."

"So would I," Legs said. "But if you want to wait for your lawyer . . ."

"My lawyer is dead, Lieutenant. *Morrie* was my lawyer. We were a team. Do you understand what that means? It was us against the world since we were fifteen years old." Leah's eyes were moist now. She was fighting back tears. "Morrie trusted no one in the whole wide world except for me. And I trusted no one but him. We fought together, side by side, for forty-seven years. And, my God, we did great things together. Not so long ago we had *four* hit shows running at once. We *ruled* Broadway. And would you like to know how we pulled it off? Because of that trust we shared. It was the one thing, the only thing, we both knew for absolute certain we could count on. It was sacred, that trust. Deep down in my heart, I knew that Morrie would never, ever lie to me. He wouldn't dare."

I nodded my head. "Until he did."

"Until he did," she acknowledged bitterly. "He sat right here and he lied to my face. Told me that R. J. Farnell was a real person and then scammed me out of my last hundred thousand. You have no idea what a betrayal that was. None. How could you?" She reached for a half-empty coffee cup on the table before her and took a sip from it. "This is cold. Are you sure you don't want me to make a fresh pot, Lieutenant? It's no trouble."

"Positive," Legs said.

"Leah, when did you learn the truth about Farnell?"

"I had my doubts about him from the very beginning. As soon as Morrie started gushing on about how many millions the man was going to invest in *Wuthering Heights*."

"How come?"

"He wouldn't let me near him, that's how come. Wouldn't let me talk to him on the phone. Wouldn't even give me the man's phone number. I had no idea how to contact him. That was *not* the way we usually did things around here. I always took care of our angels. They were my responsibility. If they had questions, I answered them. If they wanted to bitch and moan, I patted them on the head. Yet for some reason Morrie didn't trust me with Farnell. I didn't understand why. I wondered if . . ." Leah trailed off, swallowing.

"You wondered what?" Legs pressed her.

"If maybe Farnell was an associate of Joe Minetta's. If that was why Morrie didn't want me involved. It was the only thing I could think of, Lieutenant. That Morrie was laundering dirty money for some hoodlum. That's why I gave him the last of my savings. Because I was genuinely afraid for him—especially after a couple of Joe Minetta's goons came around here. It never occurred to me that Morrie had flat-out invented Farnell. And then Farnell vanished, supposedly. And Morrie hired Benji to find his girlfriend, who I knew nothing about. I'd never heard Morrie so much as mention her name until that morning you showed up here, Benji. I didn't understand what was going on. I found all of it so . . . bewildering," she confessed, wringing her hands. "That's why I went to see you at your office. Because I was so confused. After I got back here I confronted him. I said to him, 'Morrie, who is this Farnell guy? What in the hell is really going on?' And that's when he told me the truth. That he was in so deep to Joe Minetta the only option he'd had left was to run the old phantom angel scam."

"How did you feel about that?" I asked her.

"My first reaction was shock. I couldn't believe he hadn't let me know what he was doing. And then, when I realized *why* he hadn't, I got furious. I said to him, 'Morrie, you lied to my face about Farnell so you could scam me out of my money, didn't you?' He said, 'Leah, I'm in the deepest hole I've ever been in. I'm just trying to dig my way out.' I said, 'So why didn't you just *ask* me for the money?' And he said, 'Because if you knew the truth you wouldn't have given it to me.'" Leah shook her head at us in amazement. "Do you have *any* idea how many offers I had to leave him and produce my own shows? See my own name up there on the marquee? *Dozens*. But I always turned them down. Because we were a team. Because I was loyal to that man. And this was how he repaid me. By treating me with the same contempt he treated everyone else. After everything we'd been through together Morrie *used* me. I was just another sucker to him. There was no *us*. There was only *him*. You can't even begin to comprehend how devastated I was. Let me put it to you this way—when I found out that my husband, Phil, had taken up with another woman? That was a paper cut compared to what Morrie did to me. I had to go in the bathroom and throw up. After I came out I told Morrie how angry I was. And do you know what he did? He laughed at me and said, 'What's gotten into you today? Did you forget to take your estrogen or whatever the hell it is that you—you . . . ?'" Leah broke off, her chest rising and falling. "I couldn't stop stewing about it when I got home that night. The more I stewed the angrier I got. Morrie was the center of my universe. I gave my life to that man. And he betrayed that. He destroyed it."

Legs studied her curiously. "So you decided to destroy him?"

"I had to," she said quietly. "I simply could not let him get away with it. Are you sure I can't offer you gentlemen anything? A soda?"

Legs shook his head. So did I. I can't speak for Legs but I was thinking that Leah Shimmel had to be the most polite killer I'd ever come across.

"Mind you, I remained the good little soldier," she pointed out. "I followed his orders. He said, 'This stays between us. Don't show Benji your cards.' And so I didn't."

"Meaning you were playacting when I showed up here and confronted Morrie about Farnell," I said. "You weren't shocked at all to find that he didn't exist. You already knew."

"I did. I'm sorry about the charade, Benji."

"That's okay, you were following orders. And you're a pretty good actress, Leah."

"I'm a *damned* good actress. Better than half of those flighty airheads with dirty hair who I've auditioned over the years. And I had no problem doing what Morrie asked me to, because by then I'd already figured out how I was going to pay him back. Charlie and I had it all planned out."

"You recruited Charlie to help you?"

"I asked him to do me a favor. After all of the scrapes I've gotten Charlie out of he owed me one. And he was happy to help. Charlie never liked Morrie. He thought he was a nasty prick who didn't respect me. Which, as it happens, was entirely true. The basic plan was Charlie's. I can't take any credit. I simply told him that I couldn't do anything to Morrie while we were here at the office together. That would have made me the only suspect, wouldn't it?"

"Most likely," Legs acknowledged.

"So Charlie came up with what hoodlums refer to as a 'drive-by.' Lieutenant, are you . . . ?"

"I'm acquainted with the term," Legs assured her, nodding.

"The only complication Charlie foresaw was that the 'drive-by' would probably take place while Morrie was out walking on the street somewhere. That meant there'd be innocent bystanders. Therefore, I'd have to hop out of the car, shoot him at close range and then hop back in. After all, I couldn't risk hitting other people with stray bullets, could I?"

"No, you couldn't," I agreed.

"Charlie purchased the hooded sweatshirt and sweatpants for me at a sporting goods store. Also a good pair of binoculars. He got me those big sunglasses at a Duane Reade. The gun he already owned. He purchased it illegally several months ago. Charlie sells drugs from time to time on a very modest scale and he needs it for his personal protection."

"Had you fired a nine-mil before?" Legs asked her.

"Charlie showed me how," Leah responded. "Not that there was much to learn. You point and you shoot. Believe me, I found it a whole lot easier to use than my new iPhone."

"Just to be straight about this," Legs said. "Was Charlie aware that you intended to kill Morrie?"

"I told him I was going to pay Morrie back. I didn't specifically say I'd shoot him."

"But he provided you with a gun and showed you how to use it."

"Well, yes," she admitted. "And he did offer to 'blow away that fat bastard' for me, but I wouldn't let him. Morrie was *my* demon. Besides, Charlie's already been in enough trouble with the law. You'll go easy on him, won't you, Lieutenant?"

Legs thumbed his goatee for a moment. "I don't see how we can. My guess is he'll be charged as an accessory to first-degree murder. And you'll be charged with that first-degree murder."

"I'm prepared to accept the consequences for what I've done," Leah said. "I have no regrets. None. I pulled the trigger. And I handled the details. That's what I do. I take care of details. I suggested that Charlie get up early in the morning, take the subway a good distance from Williamsburg and steal the first good-sized vehicle he could find that had tinted windows. So he rode the No. 7 train out to Flushing and—"

"Stole the Navigator from a Waldbaum's parking lot," Legs said, nodding his head. "We tracked it coming into Manhattan through the Queens-Midtown Tunnel at seven minutes after ten. What did he do after that?"

"Circled around midtown until I called him. I was just waiting for Morrie to go somewhere, anywhere, so we could set our plan in motion. I needed for him to leave. Only he didn't. And then Benji showed up here to tell him that he'd discovered the truth about Farnell." Leah arched an eyebrow at me. "It was really quite remarkable the way you told Morrie off, you know. Most people didn't talk to him like that. And you look like such a little nebbish, too. After you took off, Morrie paced around here for at least another hour, making one phone call after another.

He was desperately trying to raise more money from his roster of angels. But he got nowhere, which meant he had to ask Joe Minetta for it. He phoned Joe and arranged to meet him in Bryant Park. That's when I knew I had my chance. As soon as Morrie went out the door I called Charlie and told him to meet me on the corner of 42nd Street and Sixth. Then I changed into my costume and I took off."

"My people questioned the hotel's doorman," Legs said. "How did you get out of the building without him seeing you?"

"I rode the elevator down to the basement and went out the service entrance that's used by the chambermaids and kitchen staff. And not just by them. The Morley has seen better times, sad to say. Some of its rooms these days are booked by lovers for noonday trysts. They don't necessarily want to be seen going in and out of a midtown hotel at that hour, so they slip out the service entrance. The kitchen workers are paid to look the other way. When I got up to the street I spotted Morrie halfway down the block heading toward Sixth. And I spotted you, Benji. You were following him, too."

"The job left a bad taste in my mouth. I wanted to see what his next move was." I looked at Leah curiously. "I can usually tell when I have a tail, but I didn't feel you. I wonder why."

"Possibly because I wasn't tailing you. I was tailing Morrie. And I wouldn't second-guess myself if I were you, Benji. I'm really a very efficient person when I set my mind to a specific task. Charlie was waiting for me on the corner as planned, gun in hand. I got in and we idled there, waiting for Morrie to finish his chat with Joe. I kept watch on the entrances through the binoculars. Morrie wasn't hard to spot when he came waddling out of the park. Not in that horrid green jumpsuit of his. Charlie floored it and pulled up alongside of him and I . . ." Leah paused, her mouth tightening. "I wasn't sure I'd have the nerve to do it. Shoot him, I mean. But I did. It was astonishingly easy, in fact. Because it was the right thing to do. It's never hard to do something when it's the right thing to do. Or so I've learned in my sixty-two years of living. Then I jumped back in the Navigator and we took off."

"Our security cams tracked you going down Fifth Avenue to West 37th Street," Legs said. "You made a right turn there and headed toward Sixth."

"That's correct. When we got to Sixth, Charlie went up one block to West 38th Street, pulled over and let me out."

"Were you still wearing your costume?" I asked.

"Yes, I was. And, my lord, was it hot to be wearing a hooded sweatshirt. But I didn't think it would be safe to get out of the car wearing my regular clothes. I might be observed, after all. There was an outfit waiting for me in the Navigator, folded inside a shoulder bag. I took the bag with me when I got out. Charlie headed east on West 38th Street, took the Midtown Tunnel back to Queens and ditched the Navigator somewhere. He made sure to wipe it clean of fingerprints. Then he took the subway home. He tossed the gun in a trash can somewhere along the way."

"And what did you do?"

"I strolled my way up Sixth Avenue, as planned. There are a couple of discount dress shops next to each other on Sixth just below West 40th Street. One is called Kara New York. The other is called Steps. They have racks and racks of cheap, brightly colored summer dresses. Do a very good business with young secretaries and tourists. I went in Kara New York and tried on a dress. I didn't buy it, but this gave me the opportunity to change into my own outfit unobserved. They're not allowed to have security cameras inside the dressing stalls, as I'm sure you know, Lieutenant. I stowed my costume and sunglasses in the shoulder bag and tossed it in a trashcan as I walked back here to the hotel. When the doorman greeted me he no doubt figured I'd been out running an errand. I wasn't gone very long. And I was back here in plenty of time to receive you two when you arrived with the sad news about Morrie."

"At which point you treated us to more playacting," I said. "You were very convincing in the role of the loyal assistant who was devastated by her boss's brutal murder."

"That wasn't entirely playacting, Benji. That was quite an emotional ordeal I'd just been through. And the reality was starting to sink in that Morrie was gone. Really, really gone."

"Were you feeling any regrets?" Legs asked her.

"Not a one," she answered bluntly. "I was at peace. I still am. Morrie got what he deserved. And the plan that I drew up worked to perfection."

"I have to disagree with you," Legs said. "The part about your plan working to perfection, I mean. Because it didn't, ma'am. It took Benji almost no time at all to figure out that you were Morrie's killer because, well, Benji is Meyer Golden's son. The rest of us plodding mortals would have been on to you in another day, tops. We tracked the Navigator until it made that right turn onto West 37th Street. We've been checking that whole block and it turns out there's a Marriott Fairfield Inn midway between

Fifth and Sixth. Their security cam nailed you driving by. There are cameras on Sixth that no doubt filmed Charlie dropping you off and filmed you walking into that dress shop, coming out of that dress shop and tossing your costume in the trash. We would have followed you every step of the way right back here to the Morley. Speaking of which, the Morley's own security cams will show you leaving the building by way of the service stairs. It's no good. You were never going to get away with it, don't you understand?"

Leah studied him with her alert brown eyes. "You're the one who doesn't seem to understand, Lieutenant. I don't care about what happens to me. I don't care about anything anymore."

"Not even Charlie? You roped him into helping you commit murder."

"He was happy to help. He felt useful."

"But he'll be spending a long time in jail now, thanks to you."

She looked at Legs curiously. "Have you ever met Charlie?"

"No, I haven't had the privilege yet."

"Trust me, he's much better off in prison than he is on the outside. I suppose that sounds harsh coming from his own mother. But it's the cold, hard truth. Charlie's happier on the inside. He makes friends easily. Gets plenty of exercise, has unlimited access to drugs and he doesn't have to make any decisions. Charlie does fine in prison. It's when he's on the outside that he gets into trouble."

There was a knock on the door now.

Legs opened it. Two cops in uniform stood out there in the hall. "These gentlemen will drive you to Midtown South," he told Leah before he formally arrested and informed her of her

Miranda Rights. "I really do recommend that you get yourself a lawyer."

"Thank you for your concern, Lieutenant."

"Where will we find Charlie?"

Leah glanced at her watch. "At his Thai cooking class, I believe. It's above a restaurant in Williamsburg." She gave him the address. "Please don't embarrass him in front of the others. Charlie's very sensitive. He's not a bad boy, you know. Just weak."

"We'll do our best. Now if you'll please go with these gentlemen . . ."

"Of course. Just let me get my purse and . . . will I be coming back here?"

"I'm afraid not."

"In that case I'd like to shut down my computer."

"I'll give you a hand."

He followed Leah into her office just in case she was planning to dive out a window or swallow a bottle of pills. I imagine he also went through her purse to make sure she didn't have another gun in it. They returned a moment later, Leah carrying the purse and a lightweight sweater.

She paused there for a moment, gazing around at the living room of the dingy hotel suite where she'd worked with Morrie Frankel for her entire adult life. Her eyes fell on all of those framed photos she'd been boxing up. "You'll call the folks at NYU for me, Benji?"

"Yes, I will. I'll take care of it."

"The manager can let you in. Just tell him I said it was okay."

"Will do."

"Thank you, Benji. You've been very understanding. Your mother must be extremely proud of you." Leah took one last look around, smiled at Legs and said, "I feel much better now. In fact, I haven't felt this good in years."

"In that case," he said in response, "I'm very happy for you."

A BLUE AND WHITE was double parked out front behind Legs' sedan. And Cricket was hanging around there on the sidewalk, looking guilty and miserable.

Legs and I stood under the Morley's awning and watched his men help Leah into the backseat of their blue and white. Then they got in and drove off. Leah waved good-bye to us through the window, smiling. We waved back. Neither of us was smiling.

"That was solid work you did," Legs said to me. "Your dad would have been proud."

"No, he wouldn't," I said with great certainty. "And I still don't feel like one of the good guys."

"I know you don't. That's part of the deal, I'm sorry to tell you."

"In that case I want to renegotiate."

"You don't get to. That's *not* part of the deal." He patted me on the shoulder like the big brother that he was. "Later, little bud."

"Later, Legs."

He got in his car and drove off. I started walking my way toward Sixth.

"Did Leah kill him?" Cricket hollered after me as she followed me down the block. "Is that why they're taking her in? Hey, wait up, will you, Benji?"

I stopped so that she could catch up to me. "I have nothing to say to you, Cricket."

"Come on, Benji. Be nice. I gave her up. I helped you."

"You blackmailed her into being one of your sources. And you got a girl killed."

"And I feel like shit about it. I'm incredibly sorry about what happened. It's not like I meant for it to turn out that way. I was just doing my job." Her eyes searched my face imploringly. "How do I make things right between us? Tell me, will you?"

"Well, if you want to do me a favor . . ."

"Anything. Just name it."

"If you see me walking down the street, please cross over to the other side so we don't bump into each other. I don't ever want to see you again."

Cricket gaped at me in shock. "What, just like that?"

"Just like that."

"But, Benji, I was your first sweetie."

"No need to remind me."

"And we're *friends*."

"No, we're not. Not anymore."

She glared at me now. "*You* came looking for *me* at Zoot Alors, remember? If you're searching for someone to blame you ought to be blaming yourself."

"Cricket, I'm way ahead of you on that score."

"So that's it? That's all you have to say to me?"

"No, I do have one other thing to say."

"What is it?"

"Good-bye."

"I THINK I'll have that beer now."

Farmer John's face fell when he saw me. "I wondered if you'd be back," he said, wiping the sweat from his brow with a blue bandana.

"I'm back."

Back at the Farm Project in Brownsville, where the gentle giant was sowing seeds in one of the farm's raised beds, surrounded by kids and their moms. A couple of shirtless young black guys were pushing wheelbarrows of compost around, the sweat pouring off of them. A group of teenaged girls were sneaking looks at them, whispering to one another and giggling. It was now Day Seven of the Heat Wave of the Century. The thermometer was hovering in triple digits yet again. The air was heavy and sticky. The weathermen were really, truly promising that a cold front would really, truly blow down from Canada later that night and bring mercifully fresh, cool air with it. But they'd been promising that for the past two days. I was no longer wondering if they were lying to us. I was positive they were.

Little Joe Minetta, his cousin Petey and all the other boys and girls who'd been snared in Operation Yum-Yum were out on bail. Leah Shimmel and her son Charlie had been arraigned and officially charged with the shooting death of the great Morrie Frankel. "Girl Friday Gone Wild," the geniuses at the *New York Post* had taken to calling Leah. Meanwhile, lawyers for Panorama Studios were poring over the contracts that Matthew Puntigam and Hannah Lane had signed to star in Morrie Frankel's lavish, trouble-plagued sixty-five-million-dollar musical production of *Wuthering Heights*. According to an informed source, it now appeared likely that the young stars would fly to Tanzania very soon to begin filming *The Son of Tarzan*. They hoped to resume their quest for Broadway stardom next season in a Panorama-backed production of *Wuthering Heights*.

I know this because I read it on *crickoshea.com*.

Legs had the unhappy task of contacting Boso's mother down in Ruston, Louisiana, to notify her of her daughter's death. He told me that Boso's mother took the news without emotion. He also told me that he'd had zero luck tracking down our rooftop shooter, who'd fired from the window of a vacant eighth-floor apartment across the street on Broadway. The apartment was being repainted and the building's super had mistaken the shooter for a member of the painting crew. The super described him as a white male, about forty, medium height and build. Beyond that, Legs had nothing. Because a pro leaves nothing.

"I saw those nude photos of her in the newspapers," Farmer John said to me, his voice hoarse with grief. "I—I couldn't believe it was actually her. What did she get herself into?"

"I tried to pull her out of it, John. I did my best. I'm sorry."

"Don't be, Benji. Boso wasn't a happy person. She didn't allow herself a moment of inner peace. She's found it now." He stood there for a moment, blinking back his tears, then went back to sowing his seeds.

"What's that you're planting?"

"Our fall lettuce. Lettuce doesn't like heat. The fall's perfect for it if you start your seeds now and keep them moist."

"Do you need any help?"

"You were serious about that beer?"

"Totally."

Farmer John studied me, his big jaw stuck out. "Fair enough. You see that bed of eggplant and zucchini over there?"

"Sure thing. Want me to harvest it?"

"In your dreams. The kids do the harvesting. They love it. What they don't love is weeding. That's where people like you and me come in. It's hard, painstaking work, but it's got to be done. Come on, I'll show you." He led me over to the bed, pulling a trowel from the back pocket of his cut-off overalls. "If we don't get these weeds out of here they'll steal the soil's nutrients away from the vegetables and eventually take over. They're predators. Have to be taken out by the root. Dig down until you find the root, then give it a twist and pull it out. Don't break it off. Get the whole root. Dig, twist, pull. Then toss it in that blue barrel." He handed me the trowel. "Got it?"

"Got it." I went to work with the trowel, feeling the hot sun beating down on the back of my neck.

He stayed and weeded with me for a moment, using his pocketknife to dig with. "Mind if I ask you something?"

"I don't mind."

"Did Boso say anything to you about me?"

"Yes, she did. She said that you were a great guy."

"Was she . . . What I mean is, do you think she was ever going to come back to me?"

"No, she wasn't. You were never going to see her again."

He swallowed, blinking back his tears again. "Thanks."

"For what?"

"For not bullshitting me. You're on your own now. Just keep

doing what you're doing. When you've filled the blue barrel all the way to the top you'll be in line for that beer."

"Sounds like a deal."

Farmer John stopped for a moment to chat with some small kids who were excitedly picking green beans. Then he went back to sowing his lettuce seeds, alone with his grief, while I worked on the weeds that were preying upon his eggplant and zucchini, removing them one by one. Dig, twist, pull. Dig, twist, pull. By now the sun was baking the skin on my back right through my T-shirt. But I paid little attention to it. Just focused on the weeds and on clearing them away from the healthy living things that were trying to grow there. I found myself liking this particular job. No one was trying to play me. No one was getting shot. It was just the weeds, the soil and me. As I worked I heard the kids playing. A little boy squirted a little girl with a hose and got chased for his trouble, laughing and laughing. I heard laughter all around me. I hadn't heard any laughter for quite a while. Not since the last time I was here.